1681curse/36,900 words
2/11//13

Deliver me from Evil

BY
Harley L. Sachs

A Mystery Club Series book

ISBN 9781939381323 (paperback edition)

Books by Harley L. Sachs:
Novels

Queer Company
Never Trust a Talking Horse
The Gold Chromosome
Murder by Mail (Scratch—out!)!
Ben Zakkai's Coffin
The Search for Jesse Bram
The Mystery Club Solves a Murder
The Mystery Club and the Dead Doctor
The Mystery Club and the Hidden Witness
The Mystery Club and the Serial Widow
Conspiracy!
Murder in the Keweenaw
The Lollipop Murder
Betrayal
Retribution
Burnt Out
White Slave

Collections of short fiction

Ahoy! Quarterdeck! (Irma Quarterdeck Reports)
Anna-Lena's Troll and other stories
Threads of the Covenant: The Jews of Red Jacket
Misplaced Persons

Non-Fiction

Freelance Non-Fiction Articles
The Misadventures of Cpl. Sachs
The 1957 Sachs Arctic Expedition
From Tent to Castle: Memoir of a Year-Long Honeymoon
IS
Chilly-Chilly BANG! How We Freelanced Through Europe's Coldest Winter in a VW with a Kid
Essays and Columns: 1992-2011
The Writing Life

Cartoons

Hunting the Mail Buoy and other hazards to navigation

Acknowledgements

Thanks to Marylyn Chalmers for providing me with Laurie Cabot's definitive manual on Wicca.

Chapter One

To people who had seen the public housing projects in the 1950's that later had to be torn down because of crime and neglect, the Rose Plaza retirement complex in Portland, Oregon might seem intimidating. It was four city blocks long and consisted of a twelve story main section called the Tower with a breezeway plus an extension for assisted living built over a three level garage. Connected to it by a sky bridge was an eight story luxury annex called the Heights. Inside there were literally miles of carpeted hallways, a full time job for an employee who ran the vacuum cleaner every day. The Plaza had to be kept spotless like Disney Land or it would soon look run down and neglected like those Chicago projects that failed.

With a population of over three hundred elderly and a staff of over a hundred and fifty, the Rose Plaza was a community, a virtual village, self contained, a safe retreat in a city plagued by crime. But it was not entirely safe. Burglars had managed at times to get past the security cameras, and in recent years there had been a couple of murders.

Active in the solution to those crimes was a tight little committee called the Mystery Club, a collection of amateur sleuths whose primary activity was reading cozy mysteries written by women.

The makeup and character of the Mystery Club was changing. It had only appeared to be constant. The number of women reading mysteries written exclusively by women authors hadn't changed, but the membership did over time. Viola Cartwright, nearly blind with macular degeneration, had added her sweet disposition to the Mystery Club, but when she was murdered the balance shifted. Katherine

Seller's unchecked, dominant role could be vindictive and off-putting to some who couldn't accept people for what they were. We all have our warts and wrinkles.

As for the others, Mary Higgins had retired to early Alzheimer's and a wheelchair in assisted living with her now useless gold headed cane and her fading memories of flying for the RAF in World War II. The move depressed her partner, Ann Chambers, who remained behind in her one bedroom Tower apartment. Wilma Peters, who, unable to afford bus fare, had ridden her old Raleigh three speed bicycle to the Safeway Store for day-old groceries, had simply not waked up one morning.

No one cared much or knew what became of Wilma's bicycle. A grand nephew, her only heir, quickly cleared out her studio apartment, keeping only a few family pictures, and putting trinkets and bric-a-brac in the Plaza's resale shop, a perpetual garage sale where every small item had its own story. For instance, what was the history behind the framed postal card depicting an assassinated Austrian countess? And where had the damaged jade Buddha come from?

Some objects at the resale shop had gone through several generations of buyers, returning again and again, without enough sentimental value for the heirs to keep, too pricey to simply dispose of through the Salvation Army or Goodwill. Like the Rose Plaza residents, the place fairly reeked of history, for everyone has a story. Some are heroic, some remarkable, but none are mundane. When you live to be eighty-six, well, you have a past.

The Mystery Club members were feeling a bit thin on the ground. Anne Chambers, who still got around with a walker, however feebly, seldom came to the Mystery Club meetings. With Wilma Peters gone and Mary Higgins in assisted living, they needed, pardon the expression, new blood.

Katherine Seller, known at the Plaza for her trademark berets, the color chosen to suit the mood of her day, was the self-appointed take charge chair of the Mystery Club. Wearing her red power beret, she posted a small notice on the bulletin boards of all twelve floors of the Tower and of the Heights annex. It read, simply, "Mystery book club needs new members. We read primarily cozy mysteries written by women and meet on Mondays in the computer room at 1:30 PM. Newcomers welcome." The notice didn't say the Mystery Club was for women only. That seemed unnecessary, there being so few men in the Plazas population. Except for a few exceptions, men didn't last.

Then they waited to see who might turn up.

They waited. The approach of Halloween created a palpable undercurrent of excitement at the Rose Plaza retirement complex. Some of the staff, the maids, the wait staff in the restaurant, the continuous care helpers in the assisted living wing, and the physical fitness trainers all might make an attempt at dressing up. Some of the residents posted "Happy Halloween" decorations on their doors. There might be the odd rubber bat or plastic spider decoration. Of course, there were no trick or treaters knocking on doors or roaming the hallways. It was a high security building and no one under sixty-two lived there. There were no known resident ghosts at the Rose Plaza.

Not that weren't many possible candidates. Every month someone died at the Rose Plaza retirement complex, on the average, twenty-four to thirty deaths a year. That was no surprise, for the average move-in age was eighty-two, and the average age of the residents, sometimes called inmates by the cynical, was eighty-six. Given the demographics of a country with an aging population, it was to be expected. At eighty-six everyone knows they are on borrowed time. No one had delusions of immortality. Death was an accepted fact of life. Though there might be a sense of loss when someone died, there was no lasting feeling of shock or grief. People died at the Rose Plaza and though they were briefly mourned by friends and acquaintances, their lives celebrated in ceremonies followed by cookies and coffee in the auditorium, the losses were soon replaced by new move-ins.

So no ghosts, and in spite of the paper cut out decorations, no real witches, at least, none that made themselves known. If there was any resemblance to Macbeth's witches, it could be that the makeup of the Plaza residents was like a witches' cauldron. In a cauldron of magic potions and elixirs, the addition of one toe of frog or eye of newt to the bubbling stock pot might make a subtle change in the flavor of the whole. Every new resident changed the character of the Rose Plaza, however subtly. A wrong ingredient could throw the recipe off, creating a foul after taste, but it could also add a subtle, sweet dimension, depending on.

Who might show up in response to Katherine Seller's posted ad and how would the new addition change the character of the club?

They were in luck, or so it seemed, for you can never be quite sure on a first meeting. Some people might stop in to check out the Mystery Club, not find the group simpatico, and never return. Book clubs can be a difficult dynamic. Opinions count, but not confrontations, and then there are the passive or lazy people who don't actually read the books but go on line to read the reviews and depend on the professional critics for an opinion.

The first new recruit was a tiny, self-assertive woman with an odd foreign accent, something Slavic, perhaps, or eastern European? Someone with an imagination fired up by the Halloween spirit might suggest Transylvania, the locale of Bram Stoker's *Dracula*. The newcomer introduced herself as Ursula Besette, the first name not to be shortened as Ursel or the diminutive Ushy, pet name suitable for little children or sweethearts. Ursula was a more dignified name, and she was, if anything, a dignified elderly woman with a subtle air of mystery about her.

Like any newcomer, Mrs. Besette seemed nervous and uncertain. As a first time visitor to the Mystery Club she had wondered which was the best outfit to wear. She didn't want to appear too formal, yet though the Rose Plaza was her new home, the rules she'd been given by the marketing people cautioned. This was not an informal dormitory yet more than an impersonal apartment building. It was forbidden to be seen in the hallway in a dressing gown, and no bikinis or speedos were permitted at the Plaza's swimming pool. If anything, the Rose Plaza resembled a cruise ship with all the amenities except skeet shooting off the upper deck, and of course, no seasickness. For all the ominous warnings of an eminent 7.5 earthquake, the Rose Plaza was as steady as a rock on the volcanic basalt under its foundation.

Katherine Seller thought Ursula an awkward three syllable name whose pronunciation wasn't easy to slur. Wasn't Ursula a derivative of Ursus, the bear? Katherine had long thought about how parents came to name their children. Your name was your karma, and being given an unfortunate name would be bad karma that haunted you all your life, like the daughters of the Texas Pigg family who were named Ima and Ura. Anyone who had to declare they were a pig was doomed from the start. What was the karma of being named Ursel? Something about a bear?

Ursula Besette came to the meeting carrying a decorative canvas tote, wore a many colored, homespun jerkin cinched with a belt, and had an amulet on a chain around her neck. The amulet was a metal ring encircling a five pointed star on a blue-enameled background. Spaced between the points of the star were tiny gold letters which Katherine Seller, having originally come from New York and its Jewish population, recognized as the four Hebrew letters of the Tetragrammaton, the four letters that spelled out the unpronounceable name of God, erroneously called Yaweh by the gentile uninitiated.

Katherine Seller was not a religious person. She was too cynical to take seriously the pap handed out by guest preachers at the Plaza's Sunday vespers. The topics of religion and politics were generally regarded at the Rose Plaza as taboo, for they invariably led to confrontation, argument, and hostility. If asked, Katherine would have said she felt the whole idea of original sin was an idea cooked up to coerce the gullible into a false dilemma: accept Jesus as the sole Savior from damnation or go to hell. Katherine didn't believe in hell, original sin, and as for Jesus, well, it was a nice story if you were into myths. As for any symbolism of Ursula's choice of jewelry, she mentally dismissed it as having some sentimental attachment. Everything had its history, its story. She might have picked the trinket up at some garage sale.

Roberta Nelson, however, took her Christianity seriously and regularly volunteered at her church's food program, doling out lunches for the homeless. As long as she could park in the church lot, Roberta drove her aging, white Chevy to those events. Her neck was so stiff from arthritis that she could not turn her head in traffic, and finding a parking space near the Park Blocks was a horror. It was impossible for her to look over her shoulder when trying to parallel park. The dents and scratches on the fenders of the Chevy testified to her diminished driving ability. As long as there was an easy place to park, she drove.

It was folly to keep the car, for it sometimes refused to start, and the rental in the Plaza garage was a hundred dollars a month, but giving up the car was one of those painful life passages. Everyone who lived in the Plaza had at one time given up their house as a necessary loss, followed in many instances by giving up the dog, as only service dogs could be permitted (over the objection of almost everyone). Giving up the car in a country that lived in its automobiles meant a loss of independence. What next? Assisted living? Home health care? So Roberta still clung to the car as a sort of security blanket even though she drove only to the Safeway grocery or to her church.

Roberta noticed the amulet, but saw it only as impressive costume jewelry, perhaps an antique. She didn't interpret it as having any sinister symbolism. "What an unusual pendant. Is that an heirloom?"

"No. It's just something I found at the New Age shop on Hawthorne."

Roberta, who was interested in curious objects, always poured over the oddments in the Plaza's resale shop. She put the name of the Hawthorne store in her long term memory. Perhaps there was something there she might like.

Sylvia Jessup, the mystery club's photographer, did recognize the amulet. She always carried her digital camera on a strap around her neck. People were so used to her forever snapping pictures that they had come to ignore her. Ursula, being new to the Plaza, wasn't used to Sylvia's intrusive behavior and objected when she saw her photo was being taken. "You're not putting that on Facebook, are you?" It was a warning.

Sylvia, unlike Ann Chambers, was computer illiterate. She didn't have a Facebook account and didn't know what it was. Her level of technological expertise got only as far as the removal of the memory chip in her digital camera and insertion of it at the Rite Aid drug store photo copy machine to make prints. She did keep scrapbooks of pictures taken at Plaza events and was by default the Plaza historian. Those precious albums were kept in a cupboard in the Plaza library. "Beautiful brooch," Sylvia commented, as if to distract Ursula from her objection. "It's a satanic symbol, isn't it?"

Ursula fingered the amulet. "Some people might think so."

So the brooch had come from the New Age shop on Hawthorne? What other jewelry might be found there? Did she wear it simply for its decorative value, or did she have some sinister motive? Halloween was coming, and this satanic symbol, like the cut out bats and witches decorating some of the resident doorways, was appropriate for the holiday, but only the initiates would recognize the symbolism, like a Masonic secret handshake.

Preliminaries over, Katherine Seller took charge. "Ursula, who is your favorite author?"

Ursula fingered the amulet, an unconscious gesture someone who remembered the play might compare with Captain Queeg and the ball bearings he always jiggled when nervous. Perhaps her amulet was Ursula's equivalent to the ever present worry beads constantly carried by Arabs in the Middle East. "I don't have a single favorite. I suppose it's whatever I happen to be reading at the moment."

"Which is?"

"Well." She took a deep breath as her initial hesitancy evaporated. "Just now I'm reading Jane Hitchcock's *The Witches' Hammer.*"

"Sounds like a good title for Halloween," Roberta commented.

None of the women knew Jane Stanton Hitchcock. They were familiar with books by Dorothy Sayers, P.D. James, Paretsky, and Ivanovich, books about women detectives like Quincy Milhouse and Miss Marple. They had discovered Laurie King's series about Sherlock Holmes' Jewish wife. They eschewed Ivanovich's Sylvia Plum romps as too bawdy for their taste. But they didn't know Hitchcock.

"I'm reading her on my Kindle," Ursula said with some pride. She reached into the canvas bag and took out a Kindle Fire.

Producing a Kindle from Ursula's mysterious bag was almost as shocking as if she had pulled out a smoking revolver. None of the Mystery Club ladies owned an ereader or any of the current generation of tablet gadgets. None owned an iPad. Though Sylvia, the most technological of the bunch, had a cell phone, none of the women had a clue about texting. They were not of that generation. They grew out of a time warp when if you had a telephone it was operated by a crank that woke up a live person operator and everyone had a party line open to eavesdroppers and gossips. The nearest the Mystery Club generation came to the latest gadgetry was a passing familiarity with the computers in the room where they met, at least enough to check the Tri-Met bus schedules and "surf the web" in search of book reviews.

For books they usually waited for the Multnomah County Library bookmobile visit to the Plaza. To take the #8 bus and the streetcar down to the Central Library downtown was, well, an expedition. Occasionally Katherine Seller went as far as Powell's bookstore, but carrying heavy books back to the Plaza was tiring. "Is Hitchcock's book available in the library?"

"I'm sure it is," Ursula reassured her. "If not, you can go to Amazon.com and pick up a used copy. Sometimes they are as cheap as one cent, plus shipping and handling, of course."

Roberta Nelson was curious. "Why is it called *The Witches' Hammer?*"

Ursula took a deep breath and launched into a sort of lecture mode which made the women suspect she had been a college professor when she "was someone." They were all acutely aware of a child's comment who had once asked of a retiree, "What were you when you were someone?" It was the risk of living in a society where you are what you do, and if you no longer do it you aren't any more.

"The Witches' Hammer," Ursula began, "is actually the translation of the title of a fifteenth century tract. *Malleus Maleficarum.* It's an infamous treatise on how to define, detect, and punish witches."

What a perfect book to be reading for Halloween!

As much as her arthritic neck permitted, Roberta shook her head. "There aren't any witches nowadays. Weren't they all hanged in Salem?" Then she added with a touch of self-righteousness, "or drowned."

Ursula raised her eyebrows, or rather the penciled lines that served to punctuate her expression. "Don't be so sure. I've obtained a translation of the original Latin document about witches and have it here on my Kindle. It was endorsed by a Papal bull and used as justification for the Inquisition."

Sylvia was puzzled. "I thought the Inquisition was just about Jews."

Ursula shook her head. "It was about all forms of heresy. Did you know that in the Middle Ages over a million women were burned at the stake for being witches?"

None of the women knew the Inquisition had done that. "A million women?"

"Any statement or action that fell outside the church dogma in those days was heresy. I think you should all read the Malleus tract for yourselves," Ursula said. "Don't take my word for it. I think the Inquisition is still going on, only it's more subtle now. Nobody is burning witches at the stake these days."

Katherine remembered a film clip of a Moslem mob she had seen on the television news. "Maybe not burned, but in some places women are still being stoned to death for adultery."

Ursula nodded wisely. "You're talking about Shariah law, not heresy. I suggest we all read Hitchcock's book. I haven't finished it yet, but I think it will be an eye opener even if it is popular fiction. Certainly the fifteenth century tract it is derived from is no fiction. It's historical fact."

Always the delegator, Katherine suggested, "Maybe you can order a couple of copies of Hitchcock's book for us." She had already forgotten the title.

"We could do that now," Ursula suggested, pointing to the two PC's all booted up and ready there in the room.

"Not just yet," Katherine insisted. "I'd like to see some reviews of this Hitchcock and her books first."

Ursula nodded. "Fair enough." She'd been testing the waters of the Mystery Club. Katherine, the woman in the beret, was obviously in charge. Ursula had her confidence now and wondered how far she could go with a suggestion before encountering a "yes-but" situation.

The discussion of *The Witches' Hammer* and its source had gone on without the women noticing that they were being observed by another arrival, a man who hovered uncertainly in the open doorway.

"Is this the Mystery Club?" He was a small, bald man, stooped over like Winston Churchill in his old days, spine collapsing from osteoporosis. His was the male version of a widow's hump. The couple of sticking plasters on the top of his head suggested he was being treated for skin cancer. He had either decided to shave less frequently, or had taken on the slightly grizzled look popular among macho men, an appearance tidy enough not to look shabby, but rough enough to say to the world, "This is what I am, take it or leave it, I don't care." He was wearing black slacks and a salmon colored shirt open at the neck, no tie.

"That's us," Katherine Seller said, touching her beret in a mock salute. "And you are?"

"Judge Kahane."

Now it should be noted that, though many of the Plaza residents are retired doctors, lawyers, elected officials, professors, ministers and the like, none continued to use the titles they sported in their past lives when they "were somebody." For Ira Kahane to stick to his title long after he had ceased to be a judge was a bit like Bill Clinton being addressed respectfully as "Mr. President," or some Kentucky colonel pretending to be a grand old man when in fact in Kentucky the title is honorary. Colonel Saunders, the fried chicken king, was never a colonel of anything. To hang on to an old title looked like compensation for an ego unwilling to be deflated.

Katherine asked, "Are you a mystery fan?"

Judge Kahane pursed his lips thoughtfully. "I've read all of Ludlum's blockbusters, but I'm a bit tired of courtroom dramas. Had enough of that in my time, and, you know, when an author makes a technical error I tend to throw the book in the wastebasket."

"We read cozy mysteries," Roberta said with a measure of self-righteous condescension.

"Cozy mysteries?"

Sylvia explained, "A cozy mystery doesn't have gore, foul language, or explicit sex. Books you could read to your grandchildren without being embarrassed or offensive. The Miss Marple series, for instance. Those are cozies."

"Ah." Judge Kahane smiled and nodded. "I was told something about your study group. I heard you are a bunch of Miss Marples yourselves. Something about solving a murder here in the Plaza."

Katherine smiled with smug self satisfaction. "Several."

"You make the Plaza sound like a dangerous place."

Now Ursula was curious. As a new move-in she hadn't heard of the Mystery Club's reputation for solving crimes. The people in Marketing had not mentioned murders at the Rose Plaza. That would have killed apartment sales.

Roberta tried to reassure the newcomers. "The Plaza is no more dangerous than some neighborhoods here in Portland. This is a high security building. We have had a few burglars from time to time, but no drive by shootings. No domestic violence."

At that claim Sylvia Jessup tried to interrupt with "What about Dora Reed?" but was brushed off.

Katherine overrode both of them. "This is a secure, safe place, Mr. Kahane. Not to worry."

"Glad to hear it," the Judge said. "Now what was it you were talking about when I came in? Something about a Latin tract?"

"Malleus Maleficarum," Ursula explained. "It was a source Jane Hitchcock used in her mystery *The Witches' Hammer."*

Judge Kahane looked puzzled, his thoughts turned inward in search of some fact tucked away in his memory. His face brightened with the recollection. "Ah." He chuckled. "I prosecuted a libel case once. That book-- *Malleus*

Maleficarum—was presented by the claimant as evidence."

They were all interested. "Really?"

Kahane shook his head as if dismissing the absurd. "It was a domestic business. Something about a cat that died. A woman accused a neighbor of using witchcraft to kill her cat. Simple mediation would have solved the issue, but there was a letter to the editor, then the libel suit and a counter suit. The woman who had lost the cat claimed damages. It turned into a media circus and I was caught in the middle of it."

Now all Mystery Club ears were pricked for the details.

"The only ones who benefited were the two lawyers," Kahane continued. "I wouldn't accept the *Malleus Maleficarum* as an authoritative source as it's pure bunko from 1480, if I remember correctly. It's not part of American law. It's superstitious rubbish. I ruled that since witches do not exist, calling someone a witch might be hyperbole, but it didn't constitute libel."

"But isn't that insulting?" Sylvia asked. "I wouldn't want to be called a witch."

"It's figurative speech protected by the first amendment," Kahane said with a twinkle in his eye. "If someone calls you a son of a bitch, er..." He didn't know her name.

"Sylvia."

"If someone calls you a son of a bitch, Sylvia, you'll pardon the expression, it's an impossibility. First of all, you're a woman, not a son, and your mother isn't a female dog. If I called you a fruitcake, that would be just stupid. You couldn't collect damages for that. And not for being called a witch, either."

Now Katherine was interested. A wisp of hair had crept out from under her beret and she tucked it in. "What about witchcraft?"

Kahane sighed. "There's a long history with no coherence and little foundation in reality. Take our upcoming holiday for instance. Halloween. Now it's just for children to run around dressed as pirates or ghosts or what have you begging for candy and saying trick or treat. Now there aren't even any tricks."

"When I was a girl on the farm," Roberta remembered, "the boys would knock over outhouses and other mischief, or fill a paper bag with horse manure and set it on fire on the front porch, ring the doorbell, so someone would come out and stamp it out. Make a mess. If you asked a child for a trick now, they wouldn't know what you were talking about."

"Right," Sylvia said. "Now it's all about candy and the children get hyped up on the sugar."

Ursula knew about the real Halloween. "It wasn't always about trick or treating. The holiday goes back to the Middle Ages and was called All Hallow's Eve which got shortened by degrees to Hallo'e'en, a word with two apostrophes, now just one word. It was the evening when witches were to be rooted out before All Saints Day."

Roberta went back to her first assertion. "Like I said. There are no witches. It's all bunk."

Kahane was still remembering the *Malleus Maleficarum*. "Even though there's no scientific proof of witchcraft, there is still an interest in the occult." He pointed to Ursula's amulet. "Are you a student of Kabala, Mrs...?"

"Ursula."

"Yes. Ursula. Classical name."

Sylvia asked, "What's kabala?"

Now it was Judge Kahane's turn to shift into a lecturing mode. He was turning out to be something of an authority who would be an asset for the Mystery Club discussions, at

least in the instance of Hitchcock's book *The Witches'
Hammer.* It was as if he were sitting at the bench delivering
a legal opinion and a verdict. "Kabala is Jewish mysticism.
Its primary source is the Zohar, but there's a lot of
numerology, magic numbers."

"Magic?" Now Sylvia was interested. "How is that
different from witchcraft?"

"The definition blurs. The Hebrew letters on your
amulet," Judge Kahane said, pointing at the symbolic shape
of Ursula's jewelry. "Yod, vov, hay, vov. In Hebrew every
letter is also a number, so for instance, when someone says
as a toast Lechayem, to Life, the letters in Chai yod, are also
the number eighteen, so when giving charity the number of
dollars given is often eighteen or some multiple. The number
alludes to life and, if you believe in that sort of thing, more
power. The Kabbalist tinkers endlessly with combinations
and permutations of the letters of the name of God in search
of what we might call white magic. So the Hebrew letters on
your amulet are an incantation."

Ursula nodded. "I know."

Judge Kahane obviously didn't think much of people
who dabbled in Kabala. "I hope you don't take that business
too seriously."

Ursula didn't see any danger in it. "Why not?"

"Well…" Kahane had taken a seat in one of the wheeled
chairs at the big table. Now he tilted back and put his hands
together as if in prayer. "It can be dangerous. The Kabbalists
believe that by meditation they can ascend past the seven
gates of the tree of life to the Keter, the crown, the throne of
God. If they attain that level their spirit or soul becomes one
with God. Therein lies madness. Kabala is nothing to dabble
in."

"How do you know about this?" Roberta asked. She obviously had misgiving about this strange old man and what impact he might have on the Mystery Club. Just as every new resident of the Plaza had some effect, however subtle, on the atmosphere of the retirement complex, Judge Kahane could prove to be very disturbing. Ursula might, too. Some new ingredients to the mix were beneficial, others not so.

"I'm an Orthodox Jew, but I am not a Kabbalist."

It was almost as if he had announced he was a Martian who had arrived at the Rose Plaza from a UFO. Though there were some Jewish residents at the Plaza, they were presumably secular, made a point of being low key. Arguing about religion was taboo, so who would know? A few of those Jewish residents were Holocaust survivors of a time when a Jew was best invisible. The old Nazi era joke said it all: two Jews were about to be executed by a firing squad. The first suggested, "Let's yell "down with Hitler!"" The second said, "Don't make trouble." The only indications that there were Jewish residents in the building at all were the occasional Mezuzahs discreetly fastened to the door frames of some apartments.

As for witchcraft or magic talismans, the mezuzah itself could be seen as some sort of magic charm or amulet posted to keep away the evil eye. In fact they recalled the story in Exodus and the ten plagues. Putting the blood of a sacrificial lamb on the door post was to ward off the Angel of Death, the tenth plague.

Inside each was a scroll with a paragraph from Deuteronomy. Its modern message, simply put, was to remind Jews of who they were, an affirmation of their religious and cultural identity.

Ursula defended her choice of jewelry. "Medieval symbolism interests me."

Kahane was thoughtful. To his lawyer's mind, no subtlety should go unnoticed, no flaw in logic un-remarked. What some Jewish scholars called pilpul had good application in a secular court. "There's a narrow boundary between the white magic of Kabala and the black magic of Satanism. Dangerous territory. Witchcraft, of you will."

The more Roberta thought about it, the more she shuddered. "Jewish witchcraft. Sounds creepy to me."

"More than just creepy. It's dangerous," Judge Kahane continued. "You all know Elie Wiesel, of course, the Holocaust author. He and two friends thought they could use Kabala meditation to cast a spell and do away with Adolf Hitler. One went mad and one killed himself, leaving only Wiesel."

None of the women had heard that story.

"They were teenagers then, which is part of the reason why you are not supposed to delve into Kabala before the age of forty and even then with a tutor as a restraining guide. The temptations are too great."

Katherine was curious. "Temptations?"

Kahane sighed. He was reluctant to go into the details with these women he had barely met. "Kabala might be used to unduly influence people. To gain power over others. For seduction."

That was about enough for Roberta. "And that's in *The Witches' Hammer?*" She wasn't about to delve into something metaphysical.

"Not Kabala. Hitchcock's book is a murder mystery," Ursula explained. "And the hero is a woman. Most detectives in mysteries written by women are women."

Katherine cocked her head and checked out the women at the table, and the single man. "*The Witches Hammer*. Now you have me curious. I think we'll have a lot to talk about. That OK with all of you?"

They were all in agreement, even Kahane. "It'll be a change of pace for me. Why not?"

Chapter Two

In the week that followed, Katherine did a bit of casual research to find out about the two potential new members of the Mystery Club. She found Ursula's photograph posted in the lobby along with a couple of other new residents. According to the brief posted bio, Ursula had been born in Hungary. The short paragraph confirmed Katherine's suspicion that Ursula had something academic in her background. She had taught European History at a college in California, but she had traveled widely. Her interests were reading, Medieval History, and symbology. There was no mention of whether she had ever been married.

Most of the elderly women at the Plaza were widows, some of them multiple times. There had even been a serial widow who might have been a female bluebeard.

Katherine had used her amateur detective's wiles to tap into the gossip mill in the Resale Shop and among the volunteers at the front desk. There were not many secrets that got past those two informal information centers, but they were not enough.

As for Judge Kahane, he had a choice apartment on the eighth floor of the Heights, the posh addition to the Plaza built just before the housing bubble burst. It turned out that Kahane was not a new resident, but had been on the rolls for some time, dividing his years between winters in Palm Springs to avoid the incessant Oregon rain, and summer in Portland. He also had a house at the coast, north of Newport. He must be well off to have three places. He must still drive, even at his age, or someone else drove him to the coast, there being no public transportation from Portland other than to the Spirit Mountain Indian casino.

Taking a chance with the rather unfamiliar resources of the Internet, Katherine Googled Judge Kahane and found out that though there was a notorious Meier Kahane, leader of the Jewish Defense League who had been assassinated in Brooklyn, Judge Ira Kahane, no relation, had a short biographical notice in the Wikipedia. The entry was not complete, an invitation for further information and edits duly posted, but briefly stated it said that Kahane had handed out some harsh sentences that were overturned on appeal. There had been a failed attempt to have him disbarred for overstepping his authority on the bench. In summary, he was a tough egg who was harsh and sometimes dead wrong. All that was in the past, of course, for according to the listed date of birth Kahane was ninety. He had been retired for more than twenty years.

Katherine wasn't aware that Meier Kahane and the judge did have something in common: both their names began with a K, a tradition in the Jewish priestly caste. The name code was a persistent vestige of the ancient Hebrew class system in the days of the Jerusalem Temple with Priests, Levites, and Israelites. Of course, Ira Kahane was a judge, not a priest. Judge or not, in Orthodox circles a Kohane had special status.

As for copies of Hitchcock's mystery, the Multnomah library had two, one of which was checked out, the second at the Hillsdale branch. Sylvia put in an order for mail delivery. It cost a small fee, but saved the trouble of taking the bus and streetcar down to the Central Library to pick up a copy put on hold. Ursula had her own copy on her Kindle Fire. Judge Kahane ordered a used copy from Amazon for one cent plus p&h. No point in spending more for a book to be read only once and discarded.

While they waited, Halloween was closing in. The *Oregonian* ran a popularity contest for the favorite trick or treat candy. It was a close race: M&M's, Reese's peanut butter cups and Butter Fingers running neck and neck. So much for important local news. The newspaper ads for the grocery stores, Fred Meier and Safeway, had deals, marked down club prices at the Safeway and buy two get one free, mix or match at Freddie's. Not that any trick or treaters were going to show up at the Rose Plaza. There was no point in laying on a supply of candy to give away if no one ever came.

The staff in the wellness center went the whole nine yards, spraying fake spider webs in the doorways, and taping up cutouts of bats, ghosts and witches by the water cooler and on the mirrors.

There was a carved pumpkin in the lobby with an electric light inside. Candles were forbidden for fear of fire. Seniors might light a candle and forget about it with disastrous results. The tables in the dining room of the Plaza restaurant had tiny fetal pumpkins as centerpieces.

The Plaza set up a pumpkin carving contest and people could vote on which of those displayed in the lobby they liked best.

If you chose to explore the long hallways of the twelve story Tower you'd see a variety of decorations on the apartment doors. A couple of people who had apartments at the end of the hall where there was no risk of someone tripping over them had pumpkins parked outside their doors.

On the twelfth floor, Ursula's door was different. While others were decorated with a playful sense of Halloween fun, hers was serious. She had taped a black border around the door frame and hung garlic from the door knocker. A purple, glass, eye-shaped bauble, a common symbol in the Middle

East, was taped to the door to ward off the evil eye. There was also a large, black, crucifix mounted upside down above the door knocker, covering the peephole. Then there was the smell…

The ventilation system of the Plaza was unusual. By pressurizing the hallway, air was forced under the apartment doors which had a gap at the bottom. The fresh air from the hallways entered the apartments under the doors and out through vents in the kitchens and bathrooms. But if you opened one of the apartment windows, the pressure system was defeated. Air from outside the building came in, and instead of fresh air coming in under the doors, air and odors from the apartments escaped out into the hallway. If someone were broiling fish or frying bacon with a window open, anyone passing in the hallway could smell it. If everyone cooked at once and all opened their apartment windows, the hallways would be a virtual cloud cacophony of smells—fish, bacon, lamb, and so on, which was a good reason for the building design and the admonishment to leave the windows closed.

Someone walking the twelfth floor hallway near Ursula's apartment was assaulted by a peculiar odor. It wasn't potpourri, herbs and spices warmed in a bowl, nor was it something she was cooking. It might be incense, but there were so many joy stick fragrances, it was hard for anyone without a trained, sensitive nose, to determine just what the odor was. Cinnamon? Curry? Someone who had worked in a hospital operating room might have recognized it as the smell of blood.

Just what was going on in Ursula's studio apartment?

Then there were her visitors, duly reported to Katherine Seller by Sylvia Jessup who that afternoon was volunteering at the front desk. Two weird women came to visit Ursula.

Weird in Portland is normal, but not at the Rose Plaza. While some drivers put "Keep Portland Weird" stickers on the bumpers of their cars, they were probably alluding to Portland's gay, lesbian, and transgender population. It was not so unusual to see the occasional man dressed as a woman on a Tri-Met bus, not because he was gay or a drag queen, but because, well, he liked to dress that way. Considering that some of the tween-age girls who cruised the Lloyd Center shopping mall looked like hookers in training, a man in a dress was unobtrusive, not flaunting or flirting. Nobody cared.

Add to the gender confused sub culture the population of beggars, homeless, runaway road warriors with their pit bulls camped on the sidewalks and missionaries hawking Jesus on the corner at Pioneer Square and you had Portland's version of the circus side show. Missing were Jo-Jo the Dog faced Boy and the Bearded Lady who at one time could be seen for ten cents, a tenth part of a dollar, and step right up, ladies and gentlemen. No dime needed in weird Portland, though a dollar for a copy of Street Roots peddled by homeless vendors was appreciated. Such strange people were not part of the Rose Plaza's protected refuge for the elderly.

That didn't mean that strange types never showed up, and in the case of Ursula's two visiting women, they were.

They were both dressed in studied black, wore Goth makeup, which means black eye shadow and pale face powder, heavy beads, clanking bracelets and an in-your-face body language. The taller woman carried herself in an aggressive manner, self assured and with a "don't mess with me" attitude. She was the heavy one, the word "fat" no longer Politically Correct. Her partner, which was clearly the right word, was smaller and skinny, and wore a sort of cape. It wasn't one of those South American ponchos, just a long cloth with a hole to put your head through, but wider, so it could be wrapped around, with slits for her hands to slip through and hold it shut against the wind and rain.

Both women had tattoos, the smaller one a spider on her wrist. The other woman's tattoo recalled Viking runes, a snake that encircled her neck and throat, the head meeting the tail just under her chin. In the ancient Viking culture the encircling snake represented the cycle of life. Though tattoos were a common sight in Portland, no one at the Rose Plaza had hem, not even the few World War II navy survivors.

Sylvia signed in the two visitors, gave each an ID sticker to wear while at the Plaza, and phoned Ursula to say she had two guests. Ursula said Sylvia should just send them up to the twelfth floor.

Then, when no one was likely to overhear her, she phoned Katherine. "Ursula has two visitors."

"Oh? Who are they?"

The two women had signed in on the pink visitors' sheet. Sylvia turned it around so she could read the names. "I can't make them out. Just a scribble."

"Hmm."

"Couple of strange ones."

"Did you take their picture?"

"Heavens no. I don't do that when I'm at the reception desk." She had her camera, of course, but it was in her purse.

Having a gatekeeper didn't mean the Plaza's system was like some prison but it provided a modicum of security. The building had over three hundred residents and a staff of a hundred and eighty. There was lots of traffic. It was also four blocks long, so large that it was not safe to let unidentified strangers wander the halls unchallenged. The surveillance cameras were everywhere, of course, by all the entrances and elevators. And the tapes were kept for a week, giving management and the police time to check them out in the rare case when someone broke into the garage to prowl the cars parked there.

Tina, the smiling, svelte, paid, multi-tasking receptionist at the desk could discreetly monitor all of the cameras at her console along with the telephone and computer. It was all low key, of course. People ignored the unobtrusive cameras focused on the outside entrances and the little dark bubbles mounted on the ceilings by the elevators.

The important point was that everyone was safe. This was not like some neighborhoods in Northeast Portland where people imprisoned themselves by putting fences around their property and bars on their windows. They still risked the occasional stray bullet when gang bangers sought revenge for intrusion on their territory.

Just who those visitors to Ursula were would remain, for the time being, a mystery.

Chapter Three

Ann Chambers hadn't ordered a copy of *The Witches' Hammer*, hoping to borrow one from Roberta or Katherine, but wanted an advance peek. She downloaded Amazon's free software to her computer so she could access the Kindle book list without buying a Kindle. That done, she checked the readers' reviews. There were quite a few.

Ann was surprised, for she hadn't heard of Jane Stanton Hitchcock, but that author had many fans. Some liked the book, others were disappointed. It was "over the top" one said, and another disliked the kinky sex.

Kinky sex? To Ann that didn't sound like a chaste, cozy mystery. Another reader said the book was a gothic tale. Perversion of any kind didn't appeal to Ann, even in a Halloween book. Gothic tale? That meant like *Dracula* or *Frankenstein*, didn't it?

To get a taste of the author's style and voice, Ann downloaded a free sample. Reading a free sample of a book in the leisure of one's home was better than reading a random page or two while browsing in Powell's crowded bookstore. For Ann, who got around with a walker, standing in Powell's, even if she did make what was for her a strenuous trip on the bus and streetcar, was not an option.

For now Ann decided to reserve judgment. She read the sample and liked the author's style, voice and the suspense, but she didn't like the idea of kinky sex. She wasn't into erotica. She would wait and see what the others had to say about it.

Katherine's Google research paid off. She located an old *Newsweek* Magazine "My Turn" column by Jane Hitchcock in which she described the process in which she had written

The Witches' Hammer and mentioned *Malleus Maleficarum,* the Latin tract Judge Kahane had said was brought up in that libel case, the fifteenth century document he rejected as not be relevant to US law. Hitchcock said the discovery of the tract changed her draft of the mystery novel. Hmm. Now Katherine's curiosity was aroused.

In took awhile before copies were obtained and the Mystery Club members had time to read the book. By then Ursula's odd visitors were forgotten.

When the Mystery Club convened in the Plaza computer room Ann admitted she had only read the sample pages she'd downloaded. Judge Kahane hadn't got hold of a physical copy of the book, but had downloaded it to his PC to read on the monitor. Katherine got her copy of the book from the Multnomah library and shared it with Roberta.

Ursula opened the discussion with an apology. "*The Witches' Hammer* didn't turn out as I expected," she explained. "The original *Witches' Hammer* is the popular title of the *Malleus Maleficarum*. Hitchcock's book is about a conspiratorial group trying to get hold of a witches' manual with a secret code, not the *Malleus Maleficarum*."

Katherine, who was wearing her dark green beret that afternoon, understood why. "She explained that in her "my turn" piece in *Newsweek*. I think she got distracted by the content of the old tract. It provided a motive for the conspiracy of evil men, but not for their hunt for the witchcraft manual."

Judge Kahane agreed. "And then there's the awkward, open ending at the Swiss bank."

Ursula laughed. "Yes, and which Swiss bank? Zurich is the headquarters for the gnomes of Swiss finance. She could at least have invented a name for the bank."

Nods all around, at least nods by those who had read to the end. Those who hadn't were simply puzzled.

"I've traveled all over the world," Ursula said, "and I found the hero's search for witnesses in her tracing the source of the witchcraft manual too pat."

Katherine agreed. "It's expensive to make those trips. I mean, she's not that well off. She arrives in London and asks a cab to take her from the airport to an address, just like that."

"Right. She could at least have used Google Earth to home in on the location before she left for England. Just getting into a cab is an expensive author's short cut. I wonder if Hitchcock ever took a taxi in London."

"Or Switzerland," Katherine added, "And asked the driver to wait while she conducted a long interview. It's those careless details that infuriate me. No wonder some of the reviewers panned the book."

"What I thought we were going to get," Ursula continued with her apology, "was some detail and depth about *Malleus Maleficarum*. That's powerful stuff."

Now Judge Kahane joined the discussion. "It's the war against women. Did you realize that the issues raised in that old tract are alive and well today?"

"How's that?" Roberta asked. She hadn't read anything about *Malleus Maleficarum*.

"It defines what a witch is," Kahane explained. "To those fifteenth century men, any woman who practiced contraception, abortion, or took away a man's virility, was a witch."

Roberta, no slouch, saw a connection. "That would make the people at Planned Parenthood all witches, except for the virility part. I don't get that." The tone of her voice suggested that she was opposed to Planned Parenthood. She might not think they were witches, but she was opposed, probably because of abortions. That was not something they talked about in the Mystery Club.

Sylvia was curious. "How was a witch supposed to rob a man of his virility?"

Judge Kahane laughed at the thought. "Believe it or not, they thought a witch could steal a man's penis, make it disappear, and that a witch might have a nest in a tree full of stolen penises, like some magpie collecting shiny objects."

The word "penis" made the women uncomfortable, for they had all grown up in a period when the word "pregnant' was seldom spoken. As for "vagina," never.

Even Roberta Nelson, who looked down at the table top out of embarrassment, thought the penis story was funny.

Kahane explained, "The monster female the *Malleus Maleficarum* describes is a succubus, a fanged, big breasted, sexually dangerous creature who is a menace to men, firing up their lust, and destroying them, rendering them impotent."

"No danger of that now," Ursula said with a smirk. "Now they have Viagra."

Roberta would just as soon not get into that, especially with Judge Kahane in the room, even though at ninety he didn't look like he might be obsessed with sex. It was just not a subject she cared to discuss in mixed company, or in any company for that matter.

Kahane continued, "So today we have mostly men opposed to providing women with birth control, opposed to abortion, and opposed to women having choices of how to control their own bodies. I had to deal with some nasty cases in my court."

Katherine muttered, "Men."

Judge Kahane would have added "Christian men," being an Orthodox Jew, but it would sound inflammatory. The

Jewish religion, unlike Catholicism and Islam, had a more liberal view of women's rights, including a Jewish husband's duty to satisfy a wife's sexual needs. That was in spite of his synagogue having a screen that separated women worshippers from the men in the sanctuary. The assumption was that the presence of women sitting among the men was a distraction from prayers. Orthodox Judaism still had some archaic practices in spite of a Talmudic tradition guaranteeing a woman's rights to inherit and to own property, a girl's rights to refuse an arranged marriage, and so on. Women's rights were the theme of the portion of the Talmud called Sota. It had been the topic of study for months in the Talmud class. There was no point in his pursuing those issues to the Mystery Club ladies.

"I would still like to discuss the *Malleus Maleficarum*. Ursula said, "but that's not a mystery novel written by women. Not for us here."

"I'd like to talk with you about it privately," Kahane said. "As a legal document endorsed by the Pope, it interests me."

Ursula, whose interest was in medieval history, met his offer with a nod of agreement.

"Speaking of witches," Katherine said, "the staff of the health center is putting on a Halloween party this afternoon in the auditorium."

"Sounds like a photo op," Sylvia said. "I'll be there."

Chapter four

The Plaza auditorium, which could be divided by folding walls into three meeting rooms, had been expanded to its maximum size for the event. Fake spider webs wee draped over the entrance and tables were set up with games and little contests much like the midway of a carnival. Judge Kahane, pausing in the doorway, thought at first it was the propensity of the young set of physical therapy staff for a party, but on reflection realized that there were multiple purposes to the event.

From a mental health point of view, having some fun might be a deterrent to depression, which was not uncommon among the elderly, especially those who dwelled on their ailments and the belief that their lives were essentially over.

The games of skill were practice in hand and eye coordination. Kahane didn't take part in the exercise classes meant to keep people limber and maintain their balance, falling being a major hazard for the elderly, but he did use the treadmill and the machine that was supposed to build his upper body strength.

Then there was a Halloween bingo game that used symbols such as a little picture of a ghost or a bat instead of the numbers in the traditional bingo game.

The judge tried a one hole putting game, though he had given up golf in his eighties when his arthritic shoulder made it painful to swing a club. He did well enough at that and moved on to the bingo game. He won a pair of decorated socks which he immediately gave to Roberta Nelson who'd been one item short of a full bingo row.

The highlight of the festivity was a contest for the best costume. One of the women who worked in the assisted living section came as Little Red Riding Hood, pretending to having eaten the wolf. The winner was one of he wait staff in the restaurant who came as death, his face hidden by a black hood, and carrying not the traditional scythe but a large, fake knife.

What was peculiar, the judge thought, was Roberta's reaction to one of the housekeeping staff who came as a witch. The girl's makeup was grotesque. She had someone affixed fake warts to her face, and a hooked nose. Her eye makeup was sinister. She wore the pointed witches' black hat and carried a stuffed black cat to represent the traditional "familiar." In the Middle Ages it was believed that witches had cats as companions, which led, in those superstitious days, to the eradication of cats.

What people did not realize then was that cats roaming through thatch-roofed villages kept down the rat population and it was the rats carrying fleas with bubonic plague that spread the black death. It was one of those unanticipated consequences of human activity.

Roberta Nelson, seeing the witch costumer froze.

Ursula, who had been selected as one of the judges of the contest, noticed Roberta's reaction. "Are you all right?"

Roberta hissed through clenched teeth. "I hate cats."

"Well, there's only one cat at the Plaza, and its not allowed out of the apartment." The only cat was a concession to the law about comfort animals. The Plaza also had one resident dog, too, over the protest of residents who were afraid of dogs, allergic to dander, or simply didn't want to find dog feces on the carpets or stairways.

"I hate witches, too," Roberta said.

Kahane tried to reassure her. "There are no witches. It's just a fairy tale, That *Malleus Maleficarum* tract was all bunk."

"I disagree," Ursula said. "The witch costume she's wearing is a stereotype, thanks to the *Malleus Maleficarum.* Witches aren't like that at all."

Roberta snapped, "What do you know about it?"

Ursula didn't answer at first. She and the other judges were tallying the results of their anonymous votes for best costumer. They announced the waiter who came as death was the winner. Then she turned to answer Roberta. "Wicca is a benevolent practice of ancient witchcraft. There's nothing sinister about it. I think Disney has contributed to the evil stereotype with Snow White, and then there's the Wizard of Oz and the Wicked Witch of the West. That's not what Wicca is about."

Roberta gave her a suspicious look. "You're an apologist for witches? Are you a witch yourself?"

Ursula shook her head. "I'm not a Wicca. But I'm interested in what they do."

With that Roberta turned away as if she had to put maximum distance between her and Ursula.

Kahane asked, "So you're studying Wicca?"

"I'm curious about Wicca and kabala, too," she said, fingering the pentacle amulet. "You're Jewish, aren't you? Maybe you know something about kabala. Why don't you come to my place tomorrow and we can talk about it?

Chapter five

Ursula invited Judge Kahane to her apartment for coffee. She had not invited anyone to her place since she moved in.

It was an indoor trek for a ninety year old man who was not very robust, for to get to her apartment from Kahane's eighth floor luxury apartment at the north end of the Heights addition to the Plaza meant walking to the Heights elevators, riding down to the third floor, crossing the sky bridge which connected to the second floor of the tower, then walking to the central bank of Tower elevators, riding back up to the twelfth floor, and finally the long, narrow hallway to Ursula's studio apartment. The Plaza complex was fully four city blocks long. The walk was something he hadn't thought about when he shopped for his Heights apartment. He found it tedious to walk so far inside the building just to fetch the mail. The residents using walkers and wheelchairs were at an even greater disadvantage.

Ira Kahane hesitated outside Ursula's door and smelled some sort of incense. What was it? Sandalwood? His sense of smell had declined in recent years, along with his taste. He found he needed more pepper on his food, salt being forbidden, in order to taste what he ate.

Ursula had put up serious decorations for Halloween. While others might have cut out paper bats or witches suitable for a kid's room, garlic hung from Ursula's door knocker. The inverted cross conveyed some sort of message to the initiated, as did the glass amulet to ward off the evil eye. Kahane knew that symbol. The gift shop at his synagogue also sold symbolic hands, sometimes as necklaces, also to ward off the evil eye. Those were ancient traditions that not everyone knew the origins of or understood.

People practiced all sorts of superstitions, like knocking on wood, throwing salt over their left shoulder, avoiding black cats, not opening an umbrella indoors, avoiding thirteen at table, or not walking under a ladder. All had an original reason and the practice continued even though the origin was forgotten. It was like that famous short story "The Lottery," in which people have long since forgotten why they performed an annual human sacrifice of stoning, but did it anyway.

Since the door knocker was disabled by the garlic hanging from it, Kahane knocked.

Ursula welcomed him. "Glad you could make it, Judge." She was wearing mauve slacks and a loose fitting knit sweater. She had ditched the necklace with the satanic star and Hebrew letters.

"It is a long walk. I can see why some Plaza residents have taken to riding electric scooters."

"A menace in the hallways and elevators. I've been nearly hit by a speeding scooter."

That was true. Before the Disabilities Act no one could move into the Plaza if they were not physically mobile and mentally alert. The original architects had not anticipated the crush when two wheelchairs or scooters had to cram into those small elevators.

"Might provide a lawyer like you with personal injury cases."

"I'm no longer in practice. Gave up the license years ago." Kahane looked around the studio apartment. It was what the British used to call a bed sit. Like most of the Plaza apartments it had wall to wall carpeting, in this case a pearl grey bound to require frequent cleaning to remove spots.

Ursula's single bed was made up like a settee with big pillows beside the single, large closet with mirrored doors which made the space seem less claustrophobic.

Couldn't she afford something bigger? Even a small one bedroom? This had to be no more than four hundred and fifty square feet. Kahane's spacious apartment in the Heights was four times as big, but it was more than four times as expensive.

The Rose Plaza had a buy-in fee, what Europeans called key money. It was similar to the membership fee for an exclusive country club. All it got you was a lifetime lease. You couldn't sell it. Inheritance wasn't an issue. Kahane's grandson Joel and his wife Mattie could not inherit it, either. Judge Kahane had outlived his only son, who had died of colon cancer in his sixties. What was the buy-in fee for Ursula's studio? The higher you were in the Tower, the more expensive, and if on the east side with the best view, the buy-in fee was even more. Maybe a studio was all she could afford.

The east wall was all windows with a view of the Willamette River and Mount Hood, its classic volcano shape dominating the horizon. It was a clear afternoon, and Mount Adams, Mount St. Helens, and other evidences of past volcanic activity were visible. Portland was situated on what had been at one time violent geologic change that was not over. Mount St. Helens had erupted in 1980 and Mount Hood, though dormant, still had steam vents testifying to the magma lurking underneath the snow and ice fields. A major earthquake was expected any time.

Besides the smell of incense, Ursula's apartment had some odd furnishings. Unlike Roberta Nelson who hated them, she apparently liked cats. A stylized ebony cat figurine stood on the window sill. A nearly lifelike stuffed black cat occupied a corner of the love seat sofa which faced a flat screen television set atop a wide, low bookcase. There was just room in a corner for a writing desk with a small office chair. A laptop computer showed in a half pulled out drawer.

In spite of the Plaza rule against candles, no doubt written in because some elderly had poor short term memory and might forget a lighted candle, Ursula had a thick, black candle on an impish candle holder that might belong in a game of Dungeons and Dragons.

Ursula's round table and two bent wire chairs, a step away from the corner galley, looked like they were more suitable to set outdoors in a patio. Those bent wire chairs surely could not be comfortable for longer than it took to eat a quick meal. Instead, Ursula had chosen to set out a tray on the glass-topped coffee table with a pair of coffee cups and a plate of chocolate chip cookies, plus a little bowl of Sees chocolates. "I'll get the coffee started," she said, and slipped into the one butt galley. "Just make yourself comfortable. You can shift Felix to the floor."

"Felix?"

"The cat."

Noting how lifelike it was, he picked up the stuffed cat by the scruff of its neck and put it down beside the couch. Kahane was not a cat person. He had once owned a white, English dog with a pointed muzzle people said resembled its owner. It had looked like Bull's-eye the dog in the Our Gang comedies, without the black circle painted around one eye.

What he was most interested in was Ursula's books. You can learn a great deal about a person from looking at what they read. There was not much room in the small studio apartment for books, but the book case under the television was crammed with antiquarian bound books. There were texts on symbology, medieval history, and witchcraft. There were three different editions of the bible, including, to Kahane's surprise, the Tanach, the Jewish name for the Hebrew Scriptures. Even more surprising was a copy of Aryah Kaplan's *Meditation and Kabala* and the *Zohar*, the seminal work in cabbalistic studies.

You study the *Zohar*?" he asked.

"It's difficult," she admitted. "I think to work through it you need a tutor. It's full of code words like 'splendor' which seem to have a secret definition. There's no glossary or explanation."

Kahane was familiar with the pitfalls of technical jargon. Invented as shorthand, abbreviations like WMD had no meaning for the uninitiated. For students of the *Zohar* it would be 'splendor,' for Catholics 'grace,' whatever that was. Language at best was imperfect. At worst it was unintelligible. That's what had made the law so challenging. Kahane had often remarked cynically that laws were written by lawyers not to be clear, but to be ambiguous and provide billable hours for anyone to try to interpret it.

Ursula didn't strike him as a religious person or a mystic. If you owned a copy of Karl Marx's *Communist Manifesto* that didn't make you a communist. It might only indicate an interest in economic theory. Owning a bible didn't make anyone a Christian or a Jew. Owning a book about witchcraft didn't make Ursula a witch. Did it? As for the books on kabala, that might just be a curiosity.

What he didn't notice at first was the area rug. Putting a rug over wall-to-wall carpeting was not a good idea, especially for elderly people who might trip and fall. Kahane looked down through the glass table top and realized that the area rug's design was a full size version of that satanic circle enclosing a star, only in this case without the letters of the Tetragrammaton. That was odd.

Ursula apologized, "I didn't ask if you preferred decaf."

"No problem." Kahane sipped, found the coffee too strong, and asked if she had any cream. "Unusual carpet."

"I found it in the New Age shop on Hawthorne." The Hawthorne district was one of Portland's funky neighborhoods, the location of scruffy cafes, odd boutiques, at least one palm reader, and stores selling imported goods made by Peruvian Indians.

"I seldom get over that way," Kahane said. He had kept on driving until he had a close call with a pedestrian while making a right turn at night. Though the pedestrian, a PSU student, had been wearing black clothing and was virtually invisible, the judge was unnerved by the experience and decided it was time to donate the old Volvo to Oregon Public Broadcasting and get a tax credit.

"It's an odd store," Ursula said. "They sell herbs and deal in homeopathic remedies. But they also sell things like that magic amulet I wore to the Mystery Club meeting."

"Oh." Homeopathic medicine was not Kahane's interest, though his prostate could probably benefit from something traditional and unconventional. His doctor at OHSU would probably not approve.

"The store is run by a couple of women. They call it New Age, but it's really ancient," Ursula explained.

Thinking of the amulet, Kahane joked, "Do they also sell eye of newt and toe of frog?"

Ursula knew the allusion to Macbeth. "Frogs are for Chinese medicine. I don't know about newts. Certainly there are no fingers of birth strangled babes ditch delivered."

"I would hope not."

Ursula hesitated before sitting down. The small sofa would have put them intimately side by side. Instead she opted to pull the office chair over so she could sit facing him.

Kahane noted that it was one of the limitations of life in a studio apartment. Two dinette chairs, an office chair, and a love seat sofa were as much furniture as one could cram into the studio without feeling cluttered and claustrophobic. She could seat only two at her little dinette table, or two on the love seat, but what if she had more guests than that?

There was an awkward silence broken when Ursula said, "I'm glad you were familiar with *Malleus Maleficarum*. That got me off the hook at the Mystery Club. I was presumptuous in pushing *The Witches Hammer* on them."

"I think they're glad to have you as a new member."

"I'm afraid I embarrassed…what's her name? The woman with the stiff neck."

"Roberta. Roberta Nelson, I think, who also hates cats. She has arthritis. At our age everyone has something wrong with them. Goes with the territory. We don't talk about it. People here don't like what they call organ recitals."

"You mean 'How's your gall bladder?'"

"Yes, like that." Kahane smiled at the recollection. "When people used to ask me 'How are you?' I used to tell them. They don't really want to know."

Preliminaries over, Ursula turned to *Malleus Maleficarum*. "What got you interested in that tract about witches?"

"The libel case brought up to me in the court. Then I mentioned it in Talmud class at the synagogue. The contrast in attitudes toward women was, well, so extreme we had some laughs about it. Though there is a reference in the Torah to diviners and sooth sayers, there are no witches in the Jewish tradition. And no war against women. I think that's a Catholic thing."

"It wasn't always," Ursula said. "In early Christianity there were female priests. The shift against them may have been a reaction to paganism. In Greek and Roman times women were priests. You remember the vestal virgins. Then there's a tradition of the Virgin Mary and the schism between Roman Catholicism and Eastern Orthodoxy."

Kahane knew only that the schism came about because in one branch of Christianity the mother of Jesus, as the mother of the Savior, was said to have also ascended bodily to heaven. It was the concept of a holy trinity versus the claim that adding Mary made it a quadrity, if there was such a thing. He did know that some Christian sects were opposed to "Trinitarians" and regarded that idea as a form of paganism. Multiple gods was a normal concept in pagan days. As Christianity amalgamated elements of pagan religions Juno, the goddess of love, became Mary.

To a strict Orthodox Jew it was all mishmash. Christianity was a mixture of the old Roman paganism and Judaism, Hebrew ethics and love. But what about *Malleus Maleficarum?*

Judge Kahane had no opinion one way or another about women being Catholic priests. The Episcopalians, basically Church of England created when Henry VIII couldn't get the Papal divorce he wanted, was half a step away from traditional Catholicism. Now they were going through an upheaval over women in the clergy.

He didn't want to air what might be seen as Jewish dirty linen on women's issues. The Orthodox Jews had only recently ordained a female rabbi though there were many female Reform and Conservative rabbis. His congregation still would not include women in the minyan, the quorum of ten worshippers necessary for certain prayers, and a girl having a bat mitzvah still could not stand at the bimah and read from the Torah scroll. It was an old superstition about what were once called a woman's unclean days. One could not know if a woman was having her period, so she could not touch the Torah. Judge Kahane saw such traditions as archaic and no longer politically correct. He saw himself as liberal, well, relatively so.

Kahane, in spite of being Orthodox, was miles away from the Lubovichers and the Haredi, what were sometimes derisively called the black hat Jews who would not shake hands with a woman. There were inside jokes about that, like having sex on the wedding night through a hole in the sheet. To avoid misunderstandings on a subject best reserved for insiders, he reminded Ursula, "There are two topics that are taboo at the Rose Plaza: politics and religion. Such discussions invariably end in conflicts and bad feelings."

"I didn't know that."

"It's not exactly an abridgement of your first amendment rights to freedom of speech. It's just being considerate and polite, like not using foul language."

"But we can explore these topics ourselves, under four eyes, as they say in German."

"Of course. But you must have noticed that Roberta Nelson didn't like the mention of sex at the Mystery Club."

Ursula laughed. "They're all mothers, aren't they? Roberta doesn't think babies are delivered by storks."

Kahane agreed. "For all I know she might be a closet reader of erotica. None of my business."

"That sort of prudery is what I found in that Malleus tract. Except it's men who blame women for uncontrolled obsession with sex."

Kahane hadn't read the tract with that in mind. To him it was all about identifying, judging, and punishing witches. "No doubt Freudians would have some fun with that."

Ursula leaned forward and put down her coffee cup. "Do you believe in witches?"

"Not in witches per se. But I do believe there is something like witchcraft. There is a long tradition about the evil eye. I see you have a charm on your door against the evil eye. As for the evil eye being witchcraft, I don't know what boundary separates that superstition from deliberate malice."

"The evil eye?"

"Yes." Kahane helped himself to one of the Sees chocolates, used the pause while he savored the soft center to give him time before speaking. He knew Ursula had an accent but wasn't sure from what country. "Perhaps in your home country they have that tradition. In South America if you admire someone's shirt they will give it to you. It's not that you covet the shirt, but they fear the evil eye if they do not give it to you. And a stranger may not look at a newborn baby. They are afraid it will be stolen."

"That's why we have the commandment 'Thou shalt not covet.' It's a warning against the evil eye."

Ursula admitted she had heard of such behavior, but hadn't known the reason. "But that's not witchcraft."

"No. I'd say that witchcraft would be casting a spell, cooking up a love potion, something like that."

"Or a curse."

That made Kahane nervous. "A curse? I think that's a Gypsy thing." For him that was forbidden territory. He realized they were dancing around a subject and Ursula was feeling him out to find out just how far she could go. What was she hiding? "I don't do curses."

"Oh? Are you superstitious?"

"I avoid what they called in the star wars movies 'the dark side.'"

"Then you think evil exists." It wasn't a question.

"I know there are evil people. I've seen them in my court. There are people with no conscience, sociopaths. They start out as abused children. They have never been loved. They can't relate to other people. You can see it in the eyes of some children."

"Really?"

Kahane nodded, sipped his coffee, and put down the cup. "I sometimes visited classrooms in K-12 schools. I could tell by looking into their eyes which children might turn into serial killers. Their souls are dead."

Ursula shuddered at the thought.

"But I don't believe in evil personified, as in Satan, if that's what you're getting at."

Ursula clearly saw the tract from a different point of view. "I could see evil in *Malleus Maleficarum.*"

"How's that? In the witches?"

"No. In the inquisitor. The *Malleus Maleficarum* was used as a justification for the Inquisition."

Kahane nodded. "I see what you mean. Did you ever read Dostoyevsky's *The Brothers Karamazov*?"

She hadn't.

"There's a long passage in the middle. The Grand Inquisitor is grilling a prisoner and proves by relentless reasoning, that the prisoner should be executed. The prisoner is Jesus."

"Ah." She was surprised.

"Look at it this way. You've studied *Malleus Maleficarum.* Seen through that vindictive, meticulous argument, Jesus was some sort of a magician, feeding a multitude with loaves and fishes, walking on water, raising Lazarus from the dead. All these could be used as evidence of witchcraft. Even if he didn't perform those miracles, he persuaded people that he did, perhaps by casting his spell over them. Mass hypnotism, if you will."

"That's twisted," Ursula said, shaking her head.

"But you see the logic. Read *The Grand Inquisitor* yourself and compare the style and logic of its argument with the *Malleus Maleficarum*. Dostoyevsky had it right. That was evil and so were the men who persecuted women for being witches."

"The War Against Women," Ursula mused.

"You can see that twisted logic of the Right to Lifers today," Kahane said. "Look at the reasoning: if a fertilized egg, not yet even a fetus, is a person, then aborting it is murder. If you believe in capital punishment, which I do not, by the way, the punishment for premeditated murder is death. So if a woman aborts her fetus, she is a murderer and risks the death penalty. How about that for someone who believes in the Right to Life? Does a murderer have a right to life? You'd be surprised how many such people believe abortionists should be killed."

"I see the similarity," Ursula admitted. "I bet I can get Dostoyevsky's book in my Kindle."

"No doubt. It's a classic."

"But you do not believe in the Devil. Isn't Satan in your bible?"

Kahane knew the argument. "It's a confusion between the English and the Hebrew word. Job is confronted by Satan, but the Hebrew word satan means 'the adversary,' in our parlance the devil's advocate, but the devil's advocate is not the Devil himself, but someone who takes that side of an argument. To make the leap from devil's advocate to the Devil himself is a mistake in logic. Judaism does not believe in the Devil. That's a Christian thing. I assume you are a Christian?"

Ursula nodded. "Nominally."

Kahane smiled. He was feeling pretty comfortable and confident that he wasn't going to cause bad feelings by getting into this subject with Ursula, even at the Rose Plaza. "Did you know that we Jews are believed to have horns?"

Ursula laughed, showing her crooked teeth. Her canines were longer than normal, but not at the level of fangs. It was a hereditary aberration few people other than a dentist might notice.

Kahane continued, "In the click-clack logic of *Malleus Maleficarum* and some Christians, if you weren't for Jesus you had to be for the Devil. The Devil was reputed to have horns, and Jews, being Devils—notice the leap of illogic here—had to have horns and even cloven feet. Some people believe that even today."

"Seriously?"

"Seriously. When my son was drafted in the Vietnam war the boys in his barracks stood around when he was getting ready for bed. They wanted to see his feet when he took off his combat boots."

Ursula laughed and shook her head in disbelief. "You don't have horns."

"No. And no hooves, either. Jews as devils is the same false dilemma of logic that says if you don't believe in Jesus as your personal savior you are going to hell. We Jews don't believe in hell, either. No Satan, no Hell, and we don't go to heaven after we die."

"So where do you go?"

Kahane shrugged. He didn't believe in heaven. Once you were dead you could not do anything. Being able to do good deeds was what mattered. If anything the here and now was heaven, if you made it that. "There is a tradition that at the end of days those dry bones, as in the Negro spiritual, come together and are resurrected. We may not believe that today, but the vestige of that belief remains in the prohibition against cremation. If your body is cremated, the bones cannot come back together for the life to come."

"Interesting."

Kahane nodded. "And the Nazis in the Holocaust not only murdered millions of Jews, but they deprived them of an afterlife by cremating their corpses. They were in a sense murdered twice."

"I never thought of that. So you could die twice."

"In a manner of speaking."

Ursula returned to part of their previous discussion. "And what about curses?"

"No curses." Kahane looked her earnestly in the eye. "I don't know what you're into, Ursula, with your interest in witchcraft and kabala, but be careful. No curses. A curse can come back to you. Like they say, what goes around, comes around. Project love and understanding and that's what you will get back."

"Even if you encounter evil?"

"Evil will destroy itself," Kahane said.

Chapter six

As Judge Kahane made his way back to his eighth floor apartment in the Rose Plaza Heights, he was worried. The clutter of Ursula's studio apartment was stifling. His conversation with Ursula was like talking to someone while trapped in an elevator. Coffee and chocolates not withstanding, it was like being locked in a room with a relentless interrogator. He was glad to escape.

She had learned a lot from him, but he learned nothing of her. That was the penalty for talking too much. He who talks and doesn't listen learns nothing. He had failed to sound her out, to ask her personal questions. The result was Ursula was still an enigma.

He knew she had an accent, but couldn't place the country. He should have asked her.

Once in his apartment and needing fresh air, he opened the door to his balcony and stepped out. The balcony was one of the features that sold him on the expensive Heights apartment. He had furnished it with a small plastic table and a couple of matching chairs that were easy to clean. He enjoyed sitting there on a warm summer morning while reading his copy of the New York Times. He could alternate focusing his weak eyes on the fine print of the newspaper with the wide view of the distant, dormant Oregon volcanoes. The balcony was a nice feature in the summer, but summer was over now and the long winter rains were going to leave a thick coating of grime. For the next few months he would not be spending much time on his balcony.

Judge Kahane took a deep breath. The air smelled of fallen leaves, autumn. The Portland air was damp and chilly. The city was blessed by trees that covered thirty percent of the city. Now the leaves were coming down, the sidewalks slippery with them, the street drains often clogged. There hadn't been any frost yet, which would take down the deciduous cover.

Kahane wondered how many more winters he was likely to experience. Not many. Maybe not even this one. What was Ursula playing at? If she wanted to dig into kabala she needed a guide. The tradition was that no one under the age of forty should study kabala. The risk was someone younger, less mature, might try to use kabala to secretly influence someone, to seduce someone or to land a job, manipulate the stock market. The result could be more dire than the sorcerer's apprentice who puts a spell on the mop to do his work for him and is then overwhelmed by an army of mops. Kabala was not a toy and its spiritualism was not like playing with a ouija board. Kabala was serious stuff.

It was, to the judge, a lot of mumbo jumbo. Numerology, the arranging and rearranging the magic letters that spelled the holy name were to him like some mystical sudoku, or whatever that puzzle in the newspaper was called. Except for the Kabbalist, finding the right combination, the magic number, was supposed to give you some mystical powers. The search for the ultimate permutation, to his mind, was an unhealthy delusion.

There were two aspects of Judaism that never came up in the study sessions at Kahane's Orthodox synagogue. One was kabala, the other the tradition of angels. Powell's bookstore had occasional volumes on angelology, but Kahane dismissed those as fantasies in the category of vampires and zombies. Kabala had been adopted as a fad by Madonna and other celebrities who took it on as a passing fancy without the essential background in the Judaism from which it sprung. Vampires and zombies were fantasies. Kabala was serious stuff. He found it to be sinister, as risky as tight rope walking while blindfolded. If Ursula pursued it, would she fall off? Or go, as the British expression put it, around the bend?

He had investigated kabala in a superficial way, only enough to learn about the universal tree of life, a diagram of seven gates someone meditating had to pass through to reach the keter, the crown. The tradition was that the keter was where the spirit of God resided, a great light. One of the most prominent American publishers of Judaica was the Keter press. That was no accident.

Some students of Joseph Campbell might conclude that seeing God as a great light was a throw back to sun worship. Didn't Jesus say, "I am the resurrection and the light"? Had Jesus been a Kabbalist?

Each of those seven gates or levels of kabalistic meditation was guarded by an evil angel. Again with the angels. It reminded Kahane of Kafka's short story in which a Jew is stuck, waiting forever at a gate that will never open. Kafka's Jewishness might have been questioned, but there was no doubt of the influence. Then there was that relentless logic of the accuser, the grand inquisitor, in *The Trial*, in which the protagonist victim doesn't know what he is on trial for.

The trouble with mysticism was that there were no answers, only questions. That was the mystery. If one pondered too much one could be trapped in a mental cul de sac. To ascend by meditation through all the gates of the tree of life to the keter meant to achieve oneness with God and make the logical leap from being *with* God to being God. Therein lay delusions of grandeur, madness as in "I am God."

Kahane was glad that he had chosen the law as his career, in spite of its frequent ambiguities. Though some laws were written to have built-in loopholes, platforms for billable argument, at least in criminal law most of the time the issue was clear. It could be excessively arbitrary as in those fixed sentences which he, as a judge, abhorred. Justice demanded a humane option, a plea bargain, a consideration of extenuating circumstances and a possibility of compassion Had he chosen to be a rabbi, a career that embraced Talmudic studies and logic, he would have been frustrated by the endless pilpul, the nitpicking questions and variations and discussion that could go on forever with no satisfactory conclusion. He was too practical a man for that. When he put down the gavel that was usually the end of it. Done.

Except if his sentence were appealed.

But he recognized the mystical traditions in Judaism. They could not be ignored or discounted. He had a mezuzah on his doorpost, a housewarming gift from his grandson, his only local relative. Though Orthodox, he did not touch the mezuzah, like some good luck charm, whenever he entered his apartment. As the hand written parchment scroll hidden inside the mezuzah said, it was a reminder of who he was. That was a tradition he accepted and respected. As for keeping away the angel of death, that was back in Egypt when the Hebrews were slaves. It wasn't for now.

He toyed with the idea that maybe Ursula should have a mezuzah instead of or in addition to the blue eye-like charm against the evil eye and the garlic which presumably warned vampires away. But Ursula was not Jewish. There was something enigmatic about her, even dangerous, depending on where her studies took her. Why the black candle? That was odd.

Should he try to guide her away from danger? Would he endanger himself? Can one tame a cobra? And what kind of task was that for a ninety-year old man with a lurking prostate cancer?

Chapter Seven

By coincidence, Sylvia Jessup, girl photographer as she had once playfully called herself at her first job for a small town newspaper, was again on duty at the front desk signing in visitors and phoning residents who got a package, when Ursula got another visit from those strange women.

This time there were three of them. Sylvia recognized the first two, the heavy one with an aggressive manner and the smaller, skinny one. Because it was raining again, the shorter woman had an umbrella which she shook off in the vestibule before folding it up.

The third woman was older. When she pulled back the hood of her yellow rain jacket she exposed her white hair. She had been beautiful once, but still had fine features not yet aged by frown lines. She was carrying a heavy leather bag reminiscent of the kits doctors used to carry when they made house calls.

Sylvia had the women sign in and stick "visitor" tags on their clothes. Then she phoned Ursula to tell her she had three visitors. This time Ursula opted to come down and meet them.

Eager to pass the news on to Katherine Seller, Sylvia decided to wait and observe. The three visitors took seats in the lobby and waited until Ursula emerged from the bank of elevators. Today she was wearing slacks and the same top Sylvia had seen before. She had apparently not met the white-haired woman before and was introduced.

Though Sylvia turned up her hearing aid. she could not hear what Ursula said. Her body language showed that she was taking her visitors on a tour of the Rose Plaza. They disappeared in the direction of the library and the restaurant beyond.

Sylvia wondered if Ursula had heard there was a finder's fee, a bonus if you will, for anyone who recruited a new resident. The elderly population of the Plaza lost someone every month and the vacated apartments had to be sold again to new residents. For the marketing folks it was a continuous process, urgent because they needed maximum occupancy to pay off the bonds that financed the Heights addition and general maintenance.

Sylvia didn't like the prospect of Ursula's visitors as potential neighbors. The Goth-like makeup was too weird for her. But, she reasoned, she shouldn't worry. Except for the new woman, they didn't look old enough to satisfy the age requirements of the retirement complex. You had to be at least sixty-two.

Sylvia studied the sign-in sheet and tried to decipher the crabbed handwriting of the visitors. Your handwriting was an extension of yourself and revealed your personality. A trained graphologist could deduce a great deal from a signature. Sylvia had dabbled in graphology at one time, though she no longer remembered the details.

She remembered the order of the women's names. The large woman had signed first, and her signature was large, and overlapped the space between the lines of the roster. The first letter, a C, was flamboyant and the signature ended with a show-off flourish. The woman had apparently practiced it at one time, indicating a big ego. This was someone who liked to show off and didn't stay inside the lines.

The second signature was a hasty scribble, the sign of someone who often had to sign things, the kind of dashed off endorsement you might find on a doctor's prescription.

The third, the signature of the woman in the yellow rain jacket, was written tight and small, indicating intense concentration, all the letters connected. Francis Beaumont, with the final T crossed low and centered, which was supposed to mean something Sylvia didn't remember. Restrained? Conservative?

These were three very different personalities. What did they have in common?

Sylvia wanted to know more about them. To make sure the cars parked in the Plaza lot were legitimately there and not dropped by someone wanting to walk their dog in Dunaway park across the street, all visitor's cars had to be noted on the sign-in sheet. Only the first signature on the list included the make, model, and license number of the car the women had come in, so it must belong to the big woman of the three, the one whose signature was intended to make an impression. They had all come in the same car, a Jeep SUV. Sylvia noted the license number and left the front desk to search the visitors' spaces in the Plaza parking lot. Which vehicle was it? She didn't know a Jeep from a Lexus, but the license number was all she needed.

She couldn't spot that number from the vestibule, so slipped out through the main entrance to have a look. It was cold out this morning and she had to wipe the rain from her forehead. She was wearing a thin cardigan over her blouse. Clutching her arms across her chest against the chill, Sylvia found the car in question. To her surprise, it was pink. You didn't expect a big hulk of a vehicle like that to be pink. It was one of those monsters, four wheel drive, with big tires. The rear bumper was decorated with stickers.

It was an American peculiarity to use your car to advertise your political point of view, like one that says "My kid beat up on your honor student." In this case, one sticker said, "If you oppose abortion, get a vasectomy." Sylvia liked that one. Another was "Gay is beautiful." She didn't care for that kind of self-exposure. Though Sylvia understood the political need to stand up for gay rights, she found flaunting of one's sexuality repugnant. Most surprising of all was a silhouette of a witch in flight with "Witches do it on broomsticks." Hmm.

Besides volunteering at the front desk, Sylvia also volunteered at the Plaza Library. Being naïve, at first she thought the bumper sticker was a reference to the Harry Potter books. The Plaza library didn't include J. K. Rawlings' books in the collection, but Sylvia remembered that when the Harry Potter books came out some parents objected to the idolization of witchcraft and wanted the books banned from school libraries. Librarians protested, saying that any author who could get kids, particularly boys, to read a seven hundred page book deserved praise. That Rawlings was forced to use only her initials and not her first name was a concession to the publisher's fear that boys would not read a book written by a woman.

It was that war against women that had come up in the Mystery Club discussion of *The Witches' Hammer*. What was wrong with men anyway?

Sylvia returned to the front desk. She'd learned a lot about Ursula's visitors, or thought she did. She wondered idly whether the Harry Potter books, besides being intended for children, could be classified as mysteries. They were, after all, written by a woman. No, the Mystery Club members would never get through such big books in time for the weekly meetings, and Harry Potter just wasn't appropriate fare. It was a YA book, for Young Adults, not senior citizen women.

Sylvia had heard of an Icelandic woman crime writer. She'd have to check that out. In the meantime, she was sure Katherine Seller would be interested in Ursula's visitors who came in a pink SUV.

Chapter Eight

Judge Kahane had a regular Friday night dinner at the home of his grandson Joel. Joel Kahane and his wife Mattie lived in a split level home with their five year old daughter Shayne high on the hill above Hillsdale. Hillsdale was a pleasant neighborhood whose anchors were Wilson High School and a new branch of the Multnomah Library with its remarkable, modern architecture. There was also a bagel place, drug store, liquor store, branch post office, couple of gas stations and a Whole Foods grocery store, all the amenities of a village even though it was part of greater Portland. It was also handy to the Jewish Community Center—called simply "The J"-- and the Jewish Academy parochial school where Mattie taught. The Ultra Orthodox congregation was across the street, along with a little gift shop, a source for everything Jewish.

Because Judge Kahane no longer drove, Joel picked him up in his pearl-grey Prius. As soon as Joel parked the car in the driveway, Judge Kahane got out and took his yarmulke out of his pocket. He never wore it at the Plaza, but always did when visiting his grandson and his wife.

Mattie Kahane was a convert to Judaism. It was not a concession to Joel, but a conscious decision. If they were to have children, she reasoned, they should be in a one religion home. She had plunged into her studies and was more religious than her husband. She stopped short of wearing a wig or covering her hair, as the most Orthodox did. At least she kept a kosher household. Judge Kahane could count on a beef brisket and matzo ball soup for the Sabbath dinner.

Shayne was the focal point of their lives, a rambunctious, vocal kid with curly brown hair. Judge Kahane could hardly remember the days when his own son was small. He had always been working and never adequately appreciated the presence of small children until it was too late. Always a small man and not athletic, Kahane was a poor participant in ball games. He'd had difficulty relating to his own son until later years and now that was too late. One was not supposed to outlive one's own children, an irrevocable loss, like a hole in the heart. At least he had his grandson Joel, Mattie and Shayne. Though they never said so to his face, they wanted their daughter to get to know her great-grandfather and have some memory of him after he died..

It was hard, being ninety, to bridge the gap to someone who was five. The judge didn't know how to talk to a child. No surprise that Shayne was bored at the shabbos dinner, which to her took too long. The only ritual she liked was the lighting of the traditional two candles. She was allowed to hold the match to the wicks and already knew the prayer. Brisket and zimmes—a concoction of carrots-- were not kids' food. Children preferred spaghetti or pizza.

It was only after the ritual of the candle lighting, the blessing over the challah twisted egg bread, and the obligatory glass of wine that Joel went to the next conventional step which was to ask what was new at the Rose Plaza. Not that he expected anything new at the retirement plaza full of elderly people, but one had to make conversation.

"I've joined the Mystery club," the Judge said.

Mattie was curious. "What's that?"

"It's a book group that reads only cozy mysteries written by women."

Joel shook his head. "Some sort of reverse sexism?"

"No. Turns out that most mystery novels actually are written by women."

Mattie didn't know what a cozy mystery was.

"It's one you could read to your kids without being embarrassed. No blood and gore, no foul language, and no sex."

Mattie commented, "Sounds boring."

"Change of pace for me from courtroom dramas."

Joel wasn't interested, but he had to make conversation. "So what are you reading?"

"We just finished *The Witches' Hammer*. It was almost disqualified because of some kinky sex."

Oops. Judge Kahane had stumbled into that one. Kinky sex was not a suitable topic when there was a five year old at the table. Shayne was suddenly interested. Today even five year olds were exposed to subjects Judge Kahane had no inkling of until he was twenty years old. Of course, when the judge was a child the word "pregnant" was never used and condoms were sold under the counters of drug stores for the sole purpose of prevention of venereal disease. As for male impotence, euphemistically called ED for erectile dysfunction, that was a totally taboo subject. Now it was a subject for television advertising. Judge Kahane dreaded having to explain to a child what an erection was. He was relieved when Mattie told Shayne she could be excused.

It was an awkward moment for the adults, too. Eyebrows were raised, as if, being ninety, Judge Kahane was supposed to have forgotten or didn't know about sex. It was one of those misconceptions about old people. Neither Joel nor Mattie, upset by the reference to "kinky sex", cared to ask for an explanation. Ira Kahane, embarrassed at his own misstep, was glad not to have to get into it. He changed the subject. "We also have another new member of the club. Woman named Ursula something or other."

"Oh? What about her?"

"She was the one who suggested the book about witchcraft. She also seems to be interested in kabala. Strange person. She's from some Eastern European country. I don't know which."

"Not Transylvania, I hope."

"Home of Vladi the Impaler? I don't think so. But she's superstitious, afraid of vampires and the evil eye. She even has garlic hung from her door knocker."

Joel laughed. "Does she also carry a wooden stake and a hammer? That's funny."

"I didn't see any wooden stake. But she does wear a satanic symbol."

Mattie got up from the table to clear the plates and fetch the dessert. "You think she's a witch?"

"That would be a new one for the Plaza," the Judge said. "We have a few strange people, even an old judge who wears a yarmulke on Friday nights. There are actually some Republicans, but they keep a low profile."

They all laughed. Kahane remembered the Plaza's statement of purpose. It was to provide a safe environment for the elderly and did not discriminate against any religion, race, or sexual orientation. If some of the residents were gay, nobody cared, and if Ursula were or were not a witch or a Wicca, nobody would care about that, either. It was live and let live, while they lasted, a mortality Kahane was all too aware of.

"So this Ursula," Mattie began, as she brought in a honey cake, "is she nice?"

"She's interesting. She's new to the Plaza and I think she's having trouble getting in step with her new lifestyle. If anything, she's a bit of an enigma, even to herself."

Joel cocked his head at his grandfather. "You're not getting involved with strange women at your age, are you?"

"I'm not involved with anyone or anything except my grandson and his lovely family. That's enough for me."

Mattie was curious. "This Ursula sounds interesting."

Judge Kahane nodded. "Everyone at the Rose Plaza is interesting. An author could write a novel about any one of the residents. They are a remarkable community. Much more interesting to me than the golfers in Palm Springs. I'm glad I'm spending this winter here, even with the rain."

That about killed the conversation. When one started talking about the weather there was nothing more to say. Just to keep from lapsing into utter boring trivia Judge Kahane offered, "I'll find out what I can about Ursula for you, Mattie. But in return you have to find out for me something about the Wicca religion. How about that?"

Chapter Nine

Ursula didn't show up at the next Mystery Club meeting and Judge Kahane wondered if she had decided the group wasn't for her. Perhaps she was ill or had a scheduling conflict. The Rose Plaza had more than forty committees. Besides the Mystery Club there were knitters, basket makers, table tennis fanatics, bridge players, singers, artists, gardeners, wood workers, and a number of opportunities for volunteering. Sylvia took her turn at the front desk and in the Plaza library; Roberta had her outside volunteerism at her church; Katherine tutored immigrant children at a nearby school. If anything, the Rose Plaza residents were too busy.

At the Mystery Club meeting Sylvia took advantage of Ursula's absence to comment on her strange visitors. "Imagine, a pink SUV with a bumper sticker that says 'Witches do it on broomsticks.'"

The Judge didn't like gossip. To an Orthodox Jew gossip was considered a sin. Perhaps it was related to the commandment not to bear false witness. "I don't think Ursula has a broomstick. At least I didn't see one in her apartment." He shouldn't have said that, for now the women all wanted to know the details. "We just had coffee. She's interested in Kabala."

Roberta wanted to know what Kabala was.

"It's a form of meditation," Kahane explained. "If anything, it's Jewish white magic."

Now the focus shifted to Kahane. The Mystery Club ladies didn't know anything about Jews or Judaism other than stereotypes. Jews were mysterious. None of the women ascribed to the cliché that Jews were all Christ killers, but Jews were, well, different, and being different were objects of suspicion. It took little imagination to see something sinister in this little, bald man who had passed judgment on people during his career on the bench. They wouldn't have been able to distinguish between an Orthodox Jew or a Reform, and had probably never heard of Reconstructionist, Conservative, or Humanistic Jews, the last being an oxymoron: Jews who didn't believe in God.

"Magic?" Roberta Nelson bristled at the idea. "Are there Jewish witches?"

Kahane shook his head. "I don't think so. Witches are not part of our religion."

"'Thou shalt not suffer a witch to live,'" Roberta quoted.

Kahane shook his head. There was no mistaking Roberta's hostility. "Sounds like you took that *Malleus Maleficarum* tract to heart." It was a complicated document, full of convoluted, twisted logic. He couldn't imagine anyone bothering to read it carefully or to take seriously a tract written in the fifteenth century.

If Roberta had actually read it, she wasn't admitting it. "Do you think Ursula is a witch?" Her aversion was unmistakable.

Kahane didn't believe the question was worthy of an answer.

Sylvia said, "Those weird women who visited Ursula might be witches."

Kahane raised a hand in protest. "Pardon me, but I thought we were here to discuss mystery novels, not to gossip about who is or isn't a witch." Was this how vicious rumors started? He had encountered a fair amount of false testimony in his career, caught people committing perjury, and seen how something innocuous could snowball into something violent. An argument about a card game could erupt spontaneously into murder. He had seen it, shuddered at the recollections, the lives ruined because of trivia. If Ursula had decided that the Mystery Club was not for her, perhaps that decision was justified. As the saying went, it took only one bad apple to ruin a barrel, and one nasty gossip could poison an otherwise innocuous, friendly gathering.

Kahane knew nothing of witchcraft other than the nonsense he'd found in the *Malleus Maleficarum.* In its time it had set off a fatal chain of events. The tract was propaganda used as justification for hysterical extermination of perhaps millions of women and other alleged witches.

The sequence of unfortunate results didn't end there. The belief that cats were the familiars of witches caused superstitious people to kill all the cats. The unanticipated consequence of that was the infestation of rats that carried the Black Death. It was what made that period of history a dark age. The persecution of witches and their alleged familiars had precipitated a fatal backlash.

The persecution of witches had been a fifteenth and sixteenth century phenomenon, but it was not unique. Kahane had experienced the Holocaust. Even if he had never been to Europe or survived a death camp, he knew that all Jews were survivors. The memory of the Holocaust lurked forever, not always in the background.

The fact that anyone would want to exterminate you because you weren't a Christian was never totally expunged. It wasn't like a misdemeanor that could be deleted from the court records. Didn't his synagogue have to have an armed guard at the door when they held services? The Jewish Community Center where his great granddaughter went to preschool and his granddaughter-in-law taught also had to have a guard. It wasn't paranoia. Hadn't a madman murdered people at the Seattle center? Jews could be a magnet for skinhead crazies and fanatics. It only took a spark of suspicion and hatred to trigger evil.

If Roberta Nelson and Sylvia Jessup thought Ursula was a witch terrible harm could come to the congenial atmosphere of the Rose Plaza. No thanks. "I am sure that Ursula is not a witch," Judge Kahane insisted. "Do you think she flies around on a broomstick? If you'll excuse me, that's a lot of nonsense. And even if she were a Wicca or a Moonie, it's none of our business."

That cowed them, but Kahane wasn't satisfied he had made his point. "Not that it's any of my business, but are any of you Catholic?" He realized he was infringing on a taboo here.

Katherine Seller said she had been once, but was now nothing at all.

"Look," Kahane began, trying to explain it in a way that didn't talk down to these women who, elderly they might be, were not fully wise to the world. "Some people still believe that Jews use the blood of Christian children to make matzos, even though the laws of kashrut forbid the eating or drinking of blood. That false rumor has been used to foment riots and murders of Jews. That's known as the blood libel."

The ladies of the Mystery Club were unfamiliar with the blood libel, something every Jew knew. Kahane didn't expect them to know or remember Chaucer's story about poor Hugh of Lincoln in the *Canterbury Tales*.

He pressed on, trying to explain. "Look at it this way: the Catholic Eucharist ritual calls for symbolically drinking the blood and eating the body of Christ. What if Jews were hysterical and ignorant enough to think that what was drunk in that ritual was the actual blood of Jewish children? Don't you see how incendiary that could be?"

The comparison of the blood libel to the Eucharist was a bit too much for the Mystery Club to digest. They had probably never thought about the symbolism of eating God. How odd it was that such primitive customs persisted even to the twenty-first century. It was really no different from the cannibals of New Guinea who ate the brains of dead elders to acquire their wisdom. Of course, in that instance what they acquired was not wisdom, but a brain destroying disease similar to Mad Cow.

After a pause in the hopes that his message would sink in, Kahane pleaded, "Let's have no more talk about anybody being a witch." Kahane felt that the superstitions of the witches' hammer tract were directly linked to the present day war against women. What was, in the definition of the Malleus, a witch? A woman who practiced contraception and performed abortions, both contested in the official platform of the Republican Party.

How odd it was that the idea persisted from the fifteenth to the twenty-first century, except women were no longer called witches. The civilization of modern day technology was a veneer over thinly concealed ancient prejudices. It was like putting a tuxedo on a Neanderthal and expecting social graces.

Hadn't Hitler skillfully aroused the Germans, considered the most advanced country in Europe, to barbaric mass murder? The Jews were not witches, of course. Their only crime was they chose not to worship Jesus. It was the basis of anti-Semitism.

Even though a retired judge, Kahane was cautious. He knew there were other Jews living at the Rose Plaza, but they kept a low profile, did not conspicuously sit at the same communal table in the restaurant or even reserve the private dining room to celebrate Passover.

If this nonsense about witches continued, how little would it take to set off something awful?

But as he left the meeting, he could not help worrying that if Ursula was or wasn't interested in witchcraft or kabala, she might be involved in something unhealthy or even dangerous.

Chapter Ten

Two of the three women who had come to visit Ursula were the owners of the New Age store where she had bought the amulet and the symbolic carpet. They were part of a group which worshipped secretly in Lake Oswego. When the coven assembled they didn't park broomsticks at the door, but their assorted automobiles. To the nosy neighbors it looked like an innocent Tupperware party or baby shower. No one would have suspected a coven of Wiccas.

Lake Oswego was an upscale suburb south of greater Portland, a community whose population was whiter than any part of Portland and, on a per capita basis, richer. It had grown around a small, artificial, private lake where, in spite of a state law that declared all navigable waters public, no one but a resident could launch a canoe without precipitating a protest.

There was no Wicca church, per se, but the women gathered in the private, fifties home owned by Francis Beaumont, the third woman who had come to visit Ursula. The house was her settlement in a typical divorce in which the husband takes the business and the wife gets the house and the mortgage which she can hardly pay off. Keeping her home and keeping up appearances was a stretch. She had already given up her car and took the #35 bus into Portland for rare shopping excursions. For the time being she was still holding on, well aware that some divorcees lost their houses and ended up homeless.

The meeting was the night of a full moon. Carol Wyden and her partner Hannah Peyton had arrived first and parked Carol's pink SUV in front of Francis's two car garage. They were soon boxed in by a pickup truck and a couple of nearly identical Honda Accords.

Altogether, they were thirteen, a magic number. Wearing robes they had brought with them, they gathered on the flagstone patio behind the house. It was surrounded by a high cedar hedge which shielded them from prying eyes as they gathered inside a pentacle painted on the flagstones. At the center was an ornate bird bath filled with water. The ritual was to draw the energy of the goddess from the image of the full moon reflected from the surface of the bowl.

To a stranger they might have appeared sinister. This was no satanic cult, no devil worship. Though mysterious and even menacing to those who did not understand it, there was nothing evil or sinister about it. The lives of women were in harmony with the phases of the moon.

In primitive, matriarchal cultures, the monthly periods of the tribal women were in sync. This phenomenon, which would be strange to uninformed men, was well known to women. Perhaps the pheromones of the menstrual cycle triggered a sympathetic reaction among other women of child bearing age. Though there might be a scientific explanation, the symbolism and spiritual nature of the lunar month and twenty-eight day menstrual cycle was important. Women were in tune with the phases of moon and the universe. They drew their spiritual power from it.

Whether it was magical or not was immaterial. The mutual goal was what Joseph Campbell called the mystical experience, and Arthur Koestler called the oceanic sense. There were many pathways to the oneness of God. This was theirs.

There were many ways to get with God. Meditation through kabala was one. The Eucharist was another. Dervishes might achieve it by whirling. Other tribes reached it by hyperventilating. Native Americans got high by eating magic mushrooms. All sought a similar euphoria.

That the Wiccas were thirteen was important, for group prayer is more powerful than individual meditation. Thirteen was their magic number. For the Jews it was ten, the minimum number of worshippers for a minyan without which there could be no kaddish prayer for the dead. Ten or thirteen, the collective energies were a critical mass.

After the ritual, the women gathered for wine, talk and business. The name of Ursula Besette of the Rose Plaza came up. "She's a customer at our store," Carol said. She had taken off her ceremonial robe and wore a light wool jerkin with a belt over baggy cotton slacks. Both garments were made of natural fibers. To Carol and her partner, synthetics like rayon, polyester, nylon, and blends containing them were not natural. Synthetics were unnatural, out of sync with the harmonics of the universe. "She's interested in our Craft."

One of the women asked, "Do you think she'd like to join our circle?"

Host Francis Beaumont could not afford wine for the group, but several had brought bottles. Hannah, who was still in her robe, had poured herself a goblet of red wine from a donated bottle. "I don't think she's a potential witch. I think she's afraid. She says there is some hostility against witches at the Rose Plaza."

Someone snorted, "That's nothing new."

Francis agreed. "I've met her. I think she is on the right path. We have to be cautious for her sake and for ours. There is so much intolerance in this world."

Recently married Carol and Hannah nodded. "How well we know."

There was a long silence while each of the women ruminated over the troubles they all faced in one way or another. Finally, one spoke up. "It's almost midnight. We could all benefit from some good thoughts and prayers, especially Francis. She needs help. We all know her financial situation isn't good. I think we should pray to the Moon Goddess that good fortune should come down to her."

Good fortune was something all of them could use.

Chapter Eleven

Roberta Nelson had not forgotten Ursula's mention of the New Age store where she bought the pentacle amulet and asked other members of the Mystery Club to join her on a little shopping excursion to the Hawthorne district. She had her own ulterior motives.

Roberta was the only member who still had a car, such as hers was. She owned a somewhat battered, white, nearly antique Chevy that sat in the Plaza garage draining her limited finances. Parking was a premium in the neighborhood, in fact, all over Portland, which was one of the most traffic congested cities in the United States. Street parking was a nightmare and private parking expensive. The monthly hundred dollar fee at the Plaza for a space in the secure garage was reasonable compared to other places in the neighborhood, generally in unprotected lots.

Considering the cost of parking and insurance, pro-rated by miles used, Roberta's weekly excursion to the nearby Safeway grocery cost her about fifty collars a trip.

Sylvia and Katherine no longer drove and depended on the Plaza bus for their grocery runs. They seldom used the Tri-Met system. Though Sylvia would like to sneak some candid photos of passengers on the bus, she needed more than that excuse to go out. Katherine didn't like to sit among the unwashed and sometimes unruly dregs of humanity, as she saw them. Their lives at the Rose Plaza had become insular, even isolated, so the two women were eager for a chance get out on a shopping excursion.

Roberta's aging Chevy was dirty from the dust and grime that blew in through the vents in the garage walls. Katherine, dolled up in a bright green beret and a matching scarf against the autumn chill, tried to avoid rubbing against the dirty car door. She commandeered the front seat. Sylvia sat in back with her digital camera. She had spare batteries in her purse.

As usual, Roberta had trouble getting the old Chevy to start. It needed a tune up and probably a new battery, but it seemed too much of an expense, considering how little she used the twenty year old car. Finally the engine kicked over. A great cloud of grey smoke came out of the tail pipe at first, but as the engine warmed up it ran more evenly and Roberta risked taking the car out.

Unable to turn her head, she didn't wait for a break in the traffic to make the right turn onto Sixth Avenue after stopping at the red light.

Though Katherine no longer drove, she knew the Oregon rules and impatiently reminded Roberta that a right turn after stopping at a red light was permitted. She also knew that the next intersection, a left turn onto a one way street, also permitted a turn against the light if the way was clear. Roberta hadn't known that. Few drivers did.

But Roberta knew the way down Fourth Street to the turn toward the Hawthorne Bridge. Soon they were in the funky Hawthorne district. Now where was the New Age store she was looking for?

Sylvia spotted it. "There!" and, without looking, Roberta swerved from the middle lane to grab a parking space. There was a squeal of brakes. She had cut off a driver who blew his horn in irritation and panic.

Sylvia protested, "One of these days you're going to get us all killed."

They got out of Roberta's car and gathered on the sidewalk before going in. The New age store window was obviously not dressed by a professional. It was crammed with a clutter of beads, trinkets, scarves, a couple of books, and what presumably was a cross section of the wares for sale inside.

The front door had a heavy grate mounted inside the glass and a steel plate around the lock. A yellow window sticker indicated that it was an Elder Friendly business. Another indicated membership in The Witches' Anti-Defamation League, the WADL, a variation on the ADL, the Anti-Defamation League that was organized against Anti-Semitism.

A bell above the door tinkled as they opened it and went inside. The New Age store had a peculiar odor. Some sort of incense you could find in a store selling products from India was mixed with a mustiness that might come from a poorly ventilated basement.

The glass display counter showed a variety of amulets, the Hand of Fatima, various sizes of blue charms against the evil eye, and different sizes of the pendant Ursula had worn to the meeting of the Mystery Club. In a glass case behind the counter were numerous mysterious bottles with labels like patchouli oil, styrax, lotus, orris, musk, and heliotrope oil. Among the dry ingredients were lovage root powder, red poppy flowers, strawberry leaves, damiana, Adam and Eve roots, none of which the Mystery Club members had any idea of. It was the witches' version of what, in another part of Portland, might be found in a shop for traditional Chinese medicine.

Homeopathic medicines, not requiring a prescription, weren't controlled by the FDA. Here were no controlled substances. Those might be found in shops selling medical marijuana, legal in Oregon and, across the Columbia River in Washington State, for recreational use, which was now legal but federally disputed.

There were book cases on the opposite wall displaying a collection of titles you wouldn't find in Powell's bookstore including *Witchcraft, the old Religion, The God of the Witches, The Woman's Encyclopedia of myths and Secrets,* and even a copy of the dreaded *Malleus Maleficarum.*

Hung from a rack in the corner were a few throw rugs with mysterious, symbolic designs.

Though she didn't remember their names, Sylvia recognized the two women who ran the place, Carol Wyden and her partner Hannah Peyton, as two of the three visitors who had come to see Ursula. They were wearing their Goth, white makeup as if it were part of a period costume put on for the sake of the customers. Clearly, with their makeup and tattoos, they were making a statement.

Carol, the heavy, taller partner, the one with the snake tattoo around her neck, didn't recognize Sylvia. "Can we help you find something?"

Roberta hung back silently, repelled by the atmosphere of the place. She didn't touch anything, as if she might become contaminated.

"I'm interested in the piece with the star in the center," Sylvia said." She pointed to the amulet in the show case.

"The pentacle. Very powerful symbolism," Carol explained.

"What are those funny letters between the points of the star?"

"Those are the Hebrew Tetragrammaton, the four letters that spell out the name of God."

It was oppressively warm in the store and Katherine loosened her green scarf. "Is that a Jewish thing?"

Sylvia shook her head. "If it were a Jewish symbol it would be a six pointed star, wouldn't it?"

"That's right," Carol said. "Some people see this as a Satanist symbol."

Roberta, obviously taken aback, asked, "Are you Satanists?"

"No," her partner answered. "We're Wiccas."

"Wiccas?"

"Witches," Hannah, the smaller, partner explained with an in your face attitude as if to say, you want to make something of it?

"Oh," Sylvia said, somewhat cowed.

Katherine wasn't about to be intimidated. Pointing at the pentacle amulet in the case, "One of our Mystery Club members has one of those. Ursula Besette. She said she got hers at your store."

Carol was not in a hurry to acknowledge that she and her partner knew or had visited Ursula.

"We all live at the Rose Plaza," Sylvia explained.

Now Carol was more cautious than ever, sensitive to this surprise delegation from the Plaza. "Did you come to buy something?"

Katherine feigned innocence. "We were just curious. I think I'd like to buy one of those blue eye things."

Hannah slid open the door to the display case and took out several of different sizes which she laid out. "These are traditional Middle Eastern charms against the evil eye. If you've ever been to Turkey you'd see them all over the place."

Katherine asked, "What do you do with them? Wear them? Hang them on your door?"

"You can wear them as a pendant. Or, if you like, you might consider the hand of Fatima. It's a common piece of Jewelry. Many Jewish women wear them. We have them as earrings, as well. Are you Jewish?"

"No," Katherine said. "I'm originally from Brooklyn. You never lose the accent." She pointed to one of the blue glass eyes. "I think I'll take this small one."

It came with a satin cord and could be worn around the neck. Carol asked, "Shall I wrap it?"

"No. I think I'll wear it." Katherine said and fussed with her beret and scarf while putting on the blue eye.

"How about you?" Carol asked the two other Mystery Club ladies. "Can I interest you in something?"

Sylvia shook her head politely. Roberta hung back as if she'd been asked to sell her soul to the devil himself.

Not wanting the purchase to show up on her credit card records, Katherine paid in cash. They got ready to leave. "Thank you very much," Katherine said. "You have a very unusual store." Unusual, of course, didn't necessarily mean nice.

They left the New Age lair of the Wiccas as if escaping from some forbidden place. Back in the New Age store, Carol and Hannah stood behind their counter rather apprehensively. One could never be sure if the Rose Plaza delegation might have some sinister intent.

Sylvia sensed Roberta's discomfort and tried to change the atmosphere. "There's lots to see here. Let's look around. I'm sure there's a coffee shop somewhere along Hawthorne." She held her digital camera at the ready for a few snapshots. The neighborhood was full of colorful people and opportunities for memorable pictures. Some were homeless beggars. Others were trying to sell something, like wallets made of duct tape.

They found a funky coffee shop and bakery, picked out rolls and scones from the display case, and settled in the window where they could watch the Hawthorne scene and talk about their experience in the New Age shop.

"You didn't buy anything," Katherine commented to Roberta. "I wonder why you wanted to go there."

"I wanted to see if they were doing anything illegal."

"Always the amateur sleuth," Sylvia said.

Roberta spread a bit of butter on her scone and took a bite. "If they were doing something illegal, the police should be notified."

Sylvia chided, "Being Wicca isn't illegal."

"That doesn't mean it's good."

Katherine eyed her over her coffee cup. "You think you can do something about it?"

"I'll see." But she didn't explain.

Chapter Twelve

AT the next meeting of the Mystery Club Katherine Seller tried to match the blue color of the charm against the evil eye with one of her half dozen berets. The navy blue was too dark, the robins egg blue too light. She settled on the latter and wore a solid color grey cotton blouse to set it off.

If she was expecting Ursula to notice, she was correct, for Ursula saw it at once. Ursula was again wearing the pentacle with the circled star and the Hebrew letters. With a teasing twinkle in her eye, she asked, "Are you warding off the evil eye?"

"Couldn't do any harm." Katherine said. "I bought it at the New Age store where you got yours. We had a little shopping excursion on Saturday. Roberta drove."

That surprised Ursula. "You still have a car?" She didn't add "at your age." Everyone at the Rose Plaza was elderly and some were still driving in their nineties. Considering how many got around with walkers or canes or stumbled from the effects of Parkinson's, it was surprising how full the three levels of the garage and the outdoor parking lot were. But age wasn't the issue. Infirmity was, and Roberta's handicap, her stiff neck, would require very careful driving. No wonder some old people drove well below the speed limit, much to the consternation of younger, impatient drivers. Many defensive elderly drivers simply stayed off the freeways which were congested with frustrated commuters. It was a miracle that there weren't more accidents.

"Yes." Roberta's brief reply and body language spoke of stubborn pride.

Judge Kahane observed the exchange. He was surprised that Katherine had bought the charm against the evil eye and wondered why the Mystery Club ladies had actually visited the New Age store. He was still trying to get the measure of the group. What was their motivation? Were they simply curious gossips or did they meddle in other people's business? To him, gossip was a sin. He had heard that the Mystery Club had actually solved some crimes that took place at the Rose Plaza. They fancied themselves as amateur sleuths. Perhaps, like Sherlock Holmes who grew testy when he didn't have a case to chew on, they needed something new to investigate, or were they just a gaggle of busybodies?

That could be sinister. If you looked for trouble, you might find it, or you might make some yourself. Kahane didn't like that.

He had to admit that he was curious, too, and rationalized that his reason was legitimate. Ursula was an interesting person. He sensed that she was at the edge of something. It might be caused by the change of scene. She was a new resident, and though physically moved into her twelfth floor studio apartment, her soul had not yet settled in. The Africans say that you might physically change your residence, but it takes your soul a year or two to adjust to the new surroundings. That must be the case for Ursula.

Ira Kahane didn't know why Ursula had chosen the Rose Plaza. There were many reasons. Some came to be near their children, but he didn't know if she had any. Others came because they'd reached the point where taking care of a house was simply too much work, expense, and responsibility. Some saw that their declining health put them on a track toward assisted living and the Rose Plaza, a continuous care facility whose assisted living wing was open only to previous residents, was a hedge against future dependency. He himself had taken the Plaza apartment first to be near his son who was then dying of colon cancer. But he still had his grandson Joel and Mattie and little Shayne close by. It was comforting and useful to be near family. Did Ursula have any family?

As for Ursula, if this had been high school and Ursula the new kid on the block, there might be competition among cliques about who would include her in their midst. Would she join the cheerleaders or the debating society? But this wasn't high school. Ursula didn't have to join up with anybody. She could, like some of the anonymous Plaza residents, simply retreat to her space, avoid human contact, and wait for the inevitable.

The unspoken truth was that the Rose Plaza, barring the occasional retreat to a family circle of caregivers or an Alzheimer's home, was their last earthly address.

Judge Kahane had not usually spent his entire year at the Plaza, for he alternated between the Palm Springs condo to escape the incessant Oregon rain plus an occasional summer forage to his son's, now Joel's cottage at the Oregon Coast, but he had been at least a part time resident for many years. He decided to give Ursula a personal welcome to her new community.

The Plaza had no Welcome Wagon as might be found in some communities. The marketing people did a good job of selling the place to potential residents, but that was not the same as an insider's view. After the Mystery Club session he invited Ursula to visit him at his apartment in the Heights. Since Kahane was only a rudimentary cook who would rather heat up something that his daughter-in-law Mattie had sent him home with, leftovers from a Sabbath meal, he didn't invite Ursula to dinner. He bought some muffins from the Plaza's own deli on the second floor of the Tower and made a pot of coffee.

Ursula was observant enough to notice the ornate mezuzah fastened to the doorpost of the Judge's eighth floor deluxe apartment at the north end of the Heights. He gave her the obligatory tour, which, being at the end of the building, offered views in three directions. To the north lay the skyscrapers of downtown Portland and to the east a view of Portland beyond the Willamette River. Because it was raining and overcast, there was no view of Mouth St. Helens or Mount Hood. The west side view was of homes precariously hanging on stilts on the side of the hill above South Broadway, waiting for the next earthquake to shake them down.

Kahane apologized for not setting as nice a table as she had when he was invited to her own place. He waited until his guest had nearly finished her first cup of coffee before he ventured to broach the subject of the Mystery Club. "I don't know if you are aware of it, (he almost said Ursula) but the ladies of the Mystery Club are not simply readers of mysteries written by women."

That puzzled her. "Oh?"

"They also have a reputation as amateur sleuths. They have, in fact, investigated some crimes that took place here at the Plaza. They have solved, or tried to solve, several murders."

Ursula smiled. "You mean like that African ladies' detective agency in Alexander Smith's books?"

Kahane didn't know the series.

She corrected herself. "But the author is a man, so they wouldn't know his books, even though the main character is a woman."

This wasn't going where Kahane wanted. "What I'm getting at is that the Mystery Club ladies are likely to snoop and meddle. As a sitting judge I encountered some whistle blowers. Let's say it's not wise to get into the lion's cage."

"I think I understand--- the Mafia functionary who knows too much ends up in the trunk of a car."

"It's not that dangerous here, but I think you should keep the Mystery Club women at a distance."

"You think they'll suspect that I'm a murderer or something?"

"I don't know what their motives are, but your private life is none of their business."

"I'm not sure what you mean."

"Your interest in kabala, for instance. That's quite outside their backgrounds and they might jump to unfortunate conclusions. None of us need that."

Ursula looked at him over her granny glasses. "You're warning me."

"You could call it that. If they give you any trouble, you can rely on me." It was the role of father confessor or confidant that, having been a judge, was natural to him. People's crises had been central to his life for many years, and though it was a relief to get out from under the overload of cases in the past, in retirement he sometimes missed the role. He wasn't a judge any more, but the title stuck.

There was a long pause as Ursula debated with herself about how much she wanted to share with the old man. Finally she said, "Did you know I escaped from Hungary during the 1956 revolution?"

"I know you still have an accent. I didn't place it."

Ursula launched into her own story. "You might not know, but Hungary was a police state. During World War II we were occupied by the Nazis. Then there was a nominal independent Hungarian government that spied on everyone, and finally it was the Soviets. Who was in charge didn't much matter, for everyone informed on each other, friends and neighbors. Even children informed on their parents. Everything was collected by the Secret Police. For the slightest infraction or imagined anti-government sentiment you could be thrown in jail."

Kahane hadn't been aware of that. He remembered the 1956 uprising that the United States encouraged, but failed to intervene. Probably the risk of intervention might be war with the Soviets, so the USA, for all its encouragement, stood back and the Hungarian resistance was crushed. It was seen by Hungarians as a betrayal.

"My parents were afraid to leave, but I escaped to Austria with my boy friend. Later we went to Germany. We were married, but it didn't last."

"That's too bad." Was it? He was just being politely sympathetic. He didn't need to or want to know why Ursula's marriage had failed.

Ursula shrugged. She waited while Kahane refreshed her cup from the pot, then continued. "It was a long time ago. He was too political. I was afraid of politics. With politics in Hungary one was never safe."

Kahane had known Holocaust survivors who had feared the Gestapo, but the ones he had met, whose who survived, often did so because they were protected by Christian friends, what the Yad Hashem people call Righteous Gentiles. He thought about what it meant to be safe.

"I thought I would be safe in America," Ursula said. "It takes a long time to get over those early traumas. It is like what they now call PTSD, Post Traumatic Stress Disorder. I used to have nightmares about the secret police coming to our door. Not any more."

Kahane sighed. He remembered the McCarthy days in the 1950's when one of his college economics professors lost his job because he had suggested there were some advantages to socialism. He had been denounced by a student and fired. The incident had made Kahane wary of whistle blowers who might misinterpret some off hand remark. In these days of hyper political correctness, what at one time was tolerated or ignored as locker room banter was now redefined as racial or sexual harassment and ended up in the courts, civil actions, hefty court settlements, fines, loss of employment.

Fear of communism had dissipated with the collapse of the Soviet Union. Things were different now, or were they? Back then it was communists that were the bogey man. Now, since 9/11, it was terrorists. Politicians could cash in on public fears. Now, in the name of public safety, there were surveillance cameras everywhere and NSA, the National Security Agency, could tap into all emails and phone conversations. With the so-called cloud of information storage they could collect everything.

Ursula wanted to be safe. She still carried with her that old trauma from life in Hungary. That was a very long time ago. She didn't strike Kahane as a case as serious as the new veterans from service in Afghanistan who were so damaged by PTSD that they could no longer function. "This isn't Hungary in 1956. You are safe here," Kahane said.

Yes, the Rose Plaza was safe. It was a high security building. It wasn't as secure as the court house where he had held sway as a judge. The Plaza had no metal detectors. People coming in with bags and parcels were not inspected. Unlike the situation at his synagogue, the Rose Plaza security guard was not armed. Yes, there had been an occasional break-in at the Plaza. A burglar had once been caught roaming the miles of Tower hallways trying doors to see what was unlocked, the elderly and deaf resident asleep while he rifled drawers looking for jewelry and cash. That was not, Kahane thought, what Ursula was afraid of.

"You cannot live in perpetual fear," he said.

She agreed

"And nobody here is going to denounce you to the secret police."

"I'm an old woman," Ursula said. "What's to denounce? I am not political."

"Just so. The only thing you have to worry about here is irrational gossip."

"Which gets us back to the Mystery Club."

"I think so."

Something made Ursula suddenly laugh. "What if they thought I was a witch?"

"Are you?"

"Certainly not." Ursula put down her coffee cup and frowned, her eyes focused on nothing. "Sometimes I don't know what I am."

Kahane leaned back in his chair and smiled like the old wise man of the mountain, something he sometimes felt like, being ninety, but simply being old didn't make you wise. "You're a little old for an identity crisis."

"I do not think, Judge, one is ever too old to wonder what is coming next."

Coming next? What? At the Rose Plaza? That depended on how preoccupied you were with death. If you wondered if you'd go to heaven or hell, that might cause some death's door anxiety, but Kahane didn't believe in heaven or hell. Those were not a Jewish thing. He had no anxiety about dying. When the time came, he was content and ready. Clearly, Ursula didn't share his resignation.

Chapter Thirteen

Judge Kahane got a call from his grandson's wife Mattie. "You asked about Wicca, and what I could find out about it."

Ira Kahane had forgotten the casual request he'd made at their Sabbath meal. Mattie's follow-through reinforced his assessment of her as a thorough, intellectual person. She must be an exceptional teacher at the Jewish Academy. "What did you find out?"

"I looked it up on the Wikipedia. Wicca as a new manifestation of ancient practices was actually cooked up in the nineteen twenties. Witchcraft, of course, is ancient, but Wicca is sort of new fangled. You might even call it a fad among goddess worshippers."

"Like some New Age screwball oddity?"

"I wouldn't say that. I think they are very serious, but it seems to be a do in yourself sort of business. Nothing organized like the Catholic Church, for instance. You can look it up yourself." It was an admonition by a teacher who caught him not doing his homework.

"I'll do that."

"They don't do black magic. They are sort of environmentalists who commune with the universe. Sounds pretty harmless."

"So is there a Wicca church in Portland?"

Mattie wasn't so certain about that. "There's a number you can call. Someone in Lake Oswego."

Judge Kahane smiled at the thought that straight-laced Lake Oswego, a Republican stronghold, no doubt, might be the lair of witches. "You have the number? Did you call?"

"I didn't call, but you can. Being a Wizard might suit you, grandpa. I can just see you in a pointy hat with a wand like Dumbledore in Harry Potter."

Kahane hadn't seen the movie or read any of A. K. Rawlings' books. "Dumbledore?"

"You'd have to grow a long beard for that."

"I don't think so." Beards? He was Orthodox, but not a black hat and fringed garment Kabadnik. "So what's the number?"

Mattie gave it to him and he wrote it down. He had no intention of getting involved with the local Wiccas, but Ursula might want to know more about them. For now his curiosity was satisfied. He was not going to make a study of Wicca or witchcraft. The Torah warned against soothsayers and people who had visions.

Ursula had joked, said she was not a witch, but she surprised him. He was in the lobby picking up his mail when he bumped into her. He was standing with a fistful of junk mail, most of it appeals for donations to some charity or other. "I'm a known giver," he explained to Ursula. "Give once and they sell your address to other charities. It snowballs."

"I've got something, too," Ursula said, and showed him an envelope from the WADF.

Kahane was familiar with the ADF, the Anti-Defamation League, whose purpose was to combat anti-Semitism. He had not heard of the WADF. "What is it?"

"The Witches Anti-Defamation League. I didn't tell you. After I bought that throw rug with the Pentacle design I got a visit from the women who run the New Age shop. Then they came again with their Wicca friend."

Kahane's eyes opened wide and he wrinkled his high forehead. "Let me guess. Someone from Lake Oswego?"

Ursula was astonished. "How did you know?"

"My granddaughter-in-law made some inquiries."

"Then you know Mrs. Beaumont?"

Kahane dropped some of the junk mail and used the task of picking it up to hide his embarrassment at being caught out. "No. Actually not. Who is she?"

"Francis Beaumont has a coven. They're all Wiccas."

Kahane was suddenly nervous that they might be overheard. The mail boxes were not a place for a private conversation. "So they put you on the mailing list?"

Ursula nodded. "I'm not going to join, of course."

Kahane glanced at his fistful of appeals. "No telling what sort of catalogs you'll get now. Offers for bargains on wands and potions, I suppose."

Ursula smiled. "I think it's amusing."

Her attitude refreshed him. He had been worried about her potential paranoia brought on by old trauma, but her sense of humor was a cure. "The world is a complicated place. There are all sorts of organizations. I once got on the mailing list for guns and ammo."

Besides being dunned by the ADL, Kahane was pestered by the Southern Poverty Law Center, the Hebrew University, a hospital in Jerusalem, the ACLU, some Native American school, and on and on and on. So far, the witches didn't have his mailing address.

"The Wiccas want me to come to one of their celebrations."

"Will you go?"

She shrugged. "Maybe. Can't do any harm."

"Sure they won't cast a spell on you?"

She didn't answer.

Kahane shook his head. "Just be careful. Especially if they ask you for money."

Chapter Fourteen

Judge Kahane almost skipped the next meeting of the Mystery Club, for he had not read the latest book selection, but he had nothing better to do and wanted to observe the members. He had already figured out that Mrs. Seller chose the color of her beret to suit her mood. Today it was green, and he had no idea what that meant. Full speed ahead, perhaps.

He had not met Ann Chambers before. She came in, steadied by her walker. Ann was nearly skeletal and could not have weighed a hundred pounds. She was so bent over by a so-called widow's hump from osteoporosis that she could not look up. Infirm as she was, it was no surprise that she seldom showed up for the meetings. Kahane overheard the conversation of the others who asked how her friend Mary was doing. Ira Kahane didn't know who Mary was, but gathered that Mary was in assisted living.

Ursula came in late so she could make a theatrical entrance. She swept in like a diminutive diva wearing a black cloak over a red blouse and the usually present pentacle pendant. She took the chair at the opposite end of the long table from Katherine. Kahane was well tuned into the conventions of seating. The chairs at the table ends were the power seats. Ursula was asserting herself.

After a moment of collective surprise Sylvia Jessup brazenly snapped Ursula's picture with her ever present digital camera. "What a handsome cloak!" It was said with a tinge of sarcasm, like 'where in the world would you get a thing like that?'

"I bought it at the New Age store," Ursula said. "It even has a hood, see?" She pulled it up over her head. "You think it makes me look sinister?"

Katherine pursed her lips with disapproval. "They say Keep Portland Weird. You'll fit right in."

Judge Kahane tilted back in his chair, which was one of those that swiveled and was usually parked in front of one of the computers. He was enjoying Ursula's tease of the suspicious women.

Roberta Nelson was not amused. Her white hair flared around her head like a male lion's mane. She sat stiffly and glared at Ursula, but said nothing.

"I've been invited to attend a coven," Ursula confided. "I thought I'd look the part."

The women were too shocked to respond.

Kahane wasn't tongue tied. "What sort of event is it? Do they have services?" His own frame of reference was the synagogue where you had to gather a minyan of ten men to be able to say Kaddish. At his Orthodox congregation women didn't count in the minyan.

"I'm not sure. I think it's a phase of the moon thing," Ursula said. "Phases of the moon are important to Wiccas. I looked it up. Full moon, new moon, and waning moon all have some sort of special significance. They call on the moon goddess."

Her reference to the moon, goddesses and gods put Kahane into a speculative daydream. How different Wiccas, who focused on the moon, were from sun worshippers. Many religions were sun oriented. Kahane had read Joseph Campbell and admitted that when Jesus said he was the resurrection and the light, it was a reference to the sun.

Of course, the sun was the source of all energy and life on earth. Before the electric light, the work day was locked into the rising and setting of the sun. Going back even farther, darkness was a fearful time for humans. The homo sapiens wasn't a nocturnal creature. Unlike cats and other animals used to the dark, human eyes weren't constructed to work well in near or total darkness. It was a physical limitation. Some other animals' eyes reflected light. When he still drove Kahane had seen the glow of animal eyes in the darkness.

Humans were imperfect creatures. He thought, *If we had the eyes of an eagle and a cat and the noses of a dog how much could we see and smell? Perhaps the sensory overload would be too much for our brains to process.*

Light and the sun had special significance for homo sapiens. That explained the significance of candles in religious services. Every Jewish Sabbath meal began with the ritual of candle lighting, and of course Hanukah was a festival of lights, eight nights of progressively lighting the Hanukia candelabra. Catholic and other churches used candles, too. Even Unitarian services began with the lighting of a candle.

Maybe this fascination was some sort of Jungian racial memory, Kahane thought. Through how many millennia had primitive man found comfort in the fire at night that kept the monsters at bay? How hypnotic it was, when he was at his house at the coast, now the property of his grandson Joel, when they sat around a fire on the beach, watched the flames, hypnotized by the embers. Fire and light.

In Kabala the Keter, the crown, the top of the tree of life, was the light of God. God was light. Human sun worship made sense to Kahane, but moon worship, well, that was foreign. Phases of the moon Ursula referred to, well, that was a woman thing.

He did know that strange things happened at the full moon. In Folklore that was when werewolves prowled, but in modern life emergency room hospital staff members were well aware of the increase in accidents and violent acts at the time of the full moon.

Kahane shook his head. And we thought we were civilized! In spite of all our technology, you couldn't escape the rhythms and power of nature. Maybe the Wiccas were onto something after all.

He roused himself out of his ruminating on candles and light. He realized that everyone was staring at him. Maybe they thought he'd fallen asleep. He sometimes did that. If he sat very still at a meeting for five minutes he could fall asleep. It was one of the reasons he had quit driving. He roused himself and asked the question everyone wanted the answer to. "When are you going?"

"Tonight," Ursula said.

As usual, outdoors of the Plaza computer room it was raining. "I doubt if you'd be able to see the moon tonight."

Ursula didn't know what sort of ritual the Wiccas might practice.

Roberta had been tight lipped all this time. Hostility was projected like an aura by her body language. "So what are you going to do, cast a spell on us?"

Ursula missed the anger. "What would you like? I don't know what they do. Maybe they ask for nice presents at Christmas, or solstice, or whatever. I'll see."

Katherine had had enough of that. She regained control of the meeting and turned to the book they'd selected for discussion.

Kahane hardly heard any of the discussion. He was ruminating again, this time about the Wiccas. The Lake Oswego witches sounded harmless enough to him. From what little he had gathered, it was a lot more benign than the potentially sinister pitfalls of Kabala.

When the Mystery Club meeting ended he caught Ursula in the hallway outside the elevators. "Be sure and tell me how your adventure with the Wiccas goes. It's in Lake Oswego, right?"

"Yes."

Kahane noticed that Roberta Nelson was in earshot. She was reading or pretending to read the notices on the bulletin board.. "How do you get there? By bus?"

"The number 35 goes down there," she explained, "but they're picking me up."

"Sounds interesting," Kahane said. It was the most innocuous thing he could say. He didn't want to encourage her and he wasn't about to endorse the Wicca religion, if that's what it was, and not a cult.

The only religion he really knew was Judaism, and that was complicated enough, what with so many variations. One tended to stick with the religion one grew up in. Portland had seventeen different Jewish congregations. Judaism was like a smorgasbord. You could pick and choose. If you were a lox and bagel Jew you never went to synagogue. If you were into kabad, you prayed at any moment of the day, a blessing for every occurrence, every food, kosher, parve, or fleishig. There was a prayer on seeing the sunrise, of waking up in the morning. It gave the ultra Orthodox a sense of constantly being in the presence of God, or whatever. Some people shopped around until they found the congregation they liked, and often the rabbi was the deciding factor. Kahane supposed it was the same for gentiles. If you didn't like the minister you shopped for another church. Different strokes for different folks.

After all, did it matter what you called your god if there was only one? He admitted that was liberal pap. There might be only one God, but when one religious group murdered others because they worshipped in a different manner, well, that put the whole religion thing in an unfavorable light. No wonder some people rejected all of them, became agnostics or atheists. Or Wiccas?

Kahane would call Mattie and see if he could invite Ursula to join him for the weekly Sabbath meal. He would like to hear how others responded to Ursula's quest.

Chapter Fifteen

Wh**hen Judge Kahane asked his grand-daughter-in-law if he might bring a friend to the family shabbos meal she was hesitant. It meant** planning for another mouth, setting another place at the table. "I'd like you to meet Ursula Besette. She's a new resident at the Rose Plaza. She's also in the Mystery Club."

"Oh?" Mattie was waiting for more. She didn't ask if Ursula was Jewish. Not yet.

"She's originally Hungarian. Interesting person. You remember I asked about Wicca? She's connected with the Wiccas in Lake Oswego."

"Oh? I thought maybe you had a girl friend, grandpa."

That embarrassed him. A girl friend at his age? "She's not a girl friend, Mattie. But she's a puzzle. I thought you might have some insights. She's a rather troubled person."

"Is she Jewish?" Well, she'd asked.

"I don't think so." There were ways for Jews to find out who was a co-religionist-- dropping a Yiddish word, or asking simply "MOT?" for Member of the Tribe, like Mormons asked, "LDS?" Ursula hadn't done any of that.

"Ira, I'm not a psychologist. You aren't either. What are you up to? Still adopting injured parties? "

He admitted, "No. I'm not." Mattie was referring to his days as a judge. Kahane used to try to get around the mandatory sentencing rules in cases that simply, to his mind, didn't deserve imprisonment. He'd supported half way houses and rehab programs. Locking people up for possession of a controlled substance just meant another huge incarceration expense for the state. He didn't like the high percentage of recidivism and was disappointed when one of his experiments at mercy failed. "I just thought you and Joel would be a refreshing change for her from all the wrinklies here at the Plaza. I think Mrs. Besette is getting herself into a corner she might not be able to get out of."

"You mean, she might be sucked into a cult?"

"I don't know."

"Can she eat kosher?"

"How could anyone not eat kosher? "

Mattie was already considering the menu. "Maybe she's a vegetarian. Will she eat salmon?"

"I think I saw her in our restaurant eating shrimp."

"Not in this household," Mattie said. Of course, shrimp weren't on a kosher menu. "Don't worry. Joel will come for you at the usual time. If you want to pick up a bottle of wine or something you can stop at the Hillsdale Whole Foods Market on the way here."

Good. Kahane was looking forward to an interesting evening. He wondered just went on when Wiccas got together.

Chapter Sixteen

U rsula waited in the lobby on one of the chairs facing the automatic doors. Because it was raining as usual, she was wearing her yellow Land's End Gore-Tex rain jacket with a hood. The cape she'd bought at the New Age shop as a tease for the Mystery Club women might not be appropriate for this first meeting with the Lake Oswego coven. She didn't see Roberta sitting father back beside the grandfather clock, watching.

Right on time, the big pink SUV pulled up outside. Roberta didn't wait for her visitors to come in. She made her way out the door immediately.

Roberta Nelson waited until Ursula got in the back seat of the SUV and then rushed to the Plaza door. She was in time to get the license number of the oversize vehicle as it pulled away in the rainy darkness. That pink color would be easy to follow.

She had driven her aging, white Chevy out of the garage and parked it in a guest spot near the Plaza entrance, but when she tried to start the engine again it flooded and balked. The Wicca wagon was long gone. Next time she would wait in her car with the engine running. She cursed under her breath, "Thou shalt not suffer a witch to live."

Chapter Seventeen

Ira Kahane didn't ask Ursula anything about her evening with the Wiccas while they waited for Joel to pick them up for the Sabbath dinner. Instead he filled her in on the family relationship. When you are ninety there's a good chance that you have outlived your own children. That was the case for Kahane. Joel, he explained, was his grandson. His wife Mattie had converted to Judaism before their daughter Shayne was born.

Mattie wanted her baby to be born Jewish. According to Jewish tradition, the priestly caste was patrilineal. Who was a Jew, however, was determined by the mother, matrilineal descent. It was one of those ancient traditions, a curiosity, but for good historical reasons. One always knew who the mother was, but in cases of rape, fatherhood was harder to pin down. In pogroms and wars, women were often victims, but their offspring had to be accepted.

That wasn't the case in other countries. In Korea, for instance, a baby of mixed race was a non person, not accepted, mistreated.

Did Ursula know, by the way that Elvis Presley's grandmother was Jewish, which made his mother Jewish, which made him, Jewish, too. That explained the six pointed Star of David on his grave.

Mattie had wanted to be sure there'd be no quibble if she converted after Shayne was born. Her baby would be born of a Jewish mother.

Ursula found it all rather bewildering. "You make Jews sound very mysterious," she said as Joel drove up in his hybrid.

Ira Kahane smiled. "That's what's so attractive about Judaism. It's full of these ancient curiosities and, if you like, superstitions. The whole elaborate business of kashrut is derived from a single Torah quotation, 'Thou shalt not seethe a kid in its mother's milk.' You'll have a kosher meal tonight."

"I hope you like salmon," Joel said over his shoulder.

They stopped at the Hillsdale market and bought a bottle of kosher Israeli red wine before driving up past the new library into the maze of winding, narrow streets which all have variations of the same name. Whoever named the streets in that neighborhood had little imagination. There was Westwood Drive, Westwood Lane, Westwood Street, etc. None were wide enough to be called a boulevard.

Little Shayne had been helping Mattie in the kitchen and was wearing a cute apron decorated with smurfs. She looked wide-eyed at Ursula and bluntly asked, as children will do, "Are you a witch?"

Ursula squatted down to put her face at the child's level. "No. I'm not a witch. They don't like to be called that because so many stories made them out to be evil, like the Wicked Witch of the West in The Wizard of Oz. They prefer to be called Wiccas."

"Wiccas?" Shayne had never heard of that. "Can you cast a spell?"

"No. I'm just studying Wicca. It's sort of a religion."

Mattie cautioned, "I don't think she's ready for that."

"Could I be a witch? Could I fly on a broomstick like Harry Potter?"

"I don't think so." Ursula apologized. "Harry Potter is just a story." And to Mattie and Joel, "Sorry. I didn't mean to set her off."

"It's my fault," Mattie said. "I was trying to explain to her that you were going to tell us about your adventure with the witches."

"I'm afraid it's not all that exciting," Ursula said. If she had wanted to put on a show for a bunch of children she might have worn her cape, but felt it would not be appropriate to mix Wicca with a Jewish Sabbath meal. She was not wearing her pentacle pendant, either. Best to keep things low key.

Coming to the rescue, Joel said, "We can talk about it after we eat."

They took seats at the table. Shayne waned to sit beside their guest. On her booster seat she was as tall as the diminutive Ursula. Shayne had learned the blessing over the candles and she and Mattie recited together, first the Hebrew, then "Praised be Hashem, ruler of the universe, who commanded us to light the Sabbath lights."

Ira Kahane noted that the translation had been made gender neutral, a departure from the traditional blessing. The usual wording was to praise the Lord, King of the Universe. Mattie must not be as traditional Orthodox as he'd expected. Maybe the Jewish Academy had made some concessions to the non-Orthodox and the feminist movement that called God "she."

Mattie let Shayne strike a wooden match and light the two candles.

Ursula had never attended a traditional Jewish Sabbath meal with its blessings. "The Wiccas use candles in their ceremonies, too," she said.

Judge Kahane remembered the black candle he had seen in her apartment at the Plaza. Did she use it in some ritual? Or was it just for atmosphere? Candles were, in fact, prohibited at the Plaza for fear that some senile resident would forget and set the place on fire.

Joel opened the bottle of Israeli wine they brought and used it for the blessing. Then there was the challah, twisted egg bread. Each tore off a piece for the blessing over bread.

Blessings over wine and bread were a Catholic ritual, too, except for them the bread was the holy wafer of communion and the wine represented the blood of Christ. It was one of those ways the Church adopted the rituals of Judaism for its own ends.

"What else do they do?" Mattie asked as she passed a platter of grilled salmon.

"I don't really know," Ursula said, as she took a modest portion. "I was just given an introduction. Wicca depends on meditation."

Joel asked, "You mean prayer? What do Wiccas pray to?"

"Not that simple," Ursula explained. "There's a whole routine. It's about levels of brain activity. Normally we're in Beta mode. You know, when we dream the brain activity is different. There's rem sleep. Dreamers' eye movements are active. The Wiccas consciously work at getting their minds into an alpha state so they are receptive to the universe. Some philosophers might call it listening to the music of the spheres."

"What spheres? What's a sphere?" Shayne asked through a mouthful of baked potato.

Joel explained, "People used to think the universe was like a giant clock, like a lot of big balls inside other big balls, and the stars were like holes in the balls. They explained the movement of the stars in the sky to be like spheres."

Shayne didn't get it. "That's silly."

"It's how people understood things a long time ago," Mattie said. "The most complicated machine they had then was a clock, so they compared the universe to a clock."

Joel had a different explanation. "Now astronomers know that there are many galaxies and there's black holes and stuff like that."

It was too much for the five year old to get.

Ursula tried another tack. She was not used to explaining things to children. "Did you ever see the Northern Lights?"

"Like the aurora borealis?" So the kid did know more than Ursula expected.

"There are some people who think they can hear the aurora. What the Wiccas try to do is tune their minds in to the sounds of the stars, the planets, and the moon."

"The moon doesn't make any noise," Shayne protested.

Ursula shook her head. "Not noise like we hear with our ears. You know dogs can hear things we can't. And whales, too. What the Wiccas do is listen to the rhythms of the universe and tap into that energy. That's where they get their power."

Wide-eyed, Shayne asked, "Can you do that?"

"Not yet. I'm trying. I think it takes a lot of practice."

That seemed to make sense to Shayne. It did to Judge Kahane. "It sounds to me a bit like Kabala."

"Maybe it is," Ursula mused. "It's all meditation, isn't it?"

Judge Kahane thought about that. How similar meditation was to prayer. And weren't the learned rituals of prayer intended to be a routine to get in the right frame of mind? One should be able to commune with God, which was his own frame of reference. For the Wiccas it was something similar, but foreign to him. It was too heavy a subject for dinner conversation. He would have to talk with Ursula more about that alpha mental state and the steps the Wiccas used to attain it.

So what if the Wiccas did tune in to the music of the spheres, or to the power of the moon, what then?

"Have you heard of Aryah Kaplan?" Mattie asked. "I can lend you a copy of his *Jewish Meditation.*"

"I have his *Meditation and Kabala.*"

The Judge remembered seeing that on her book shelf.

"This should be a good complement to that," Mattie suggested. "I think meditation is a good method to clear the mind, to get rid of extraneous thoughts and stress. We need to get centered."

Ursula admitted, "Maybe that's what I need, to get centered."

Mediation, witches, and kabala were all outside Joel's purview. "I think this is a bit heavy for Shayne." He changed the subject. "Have some kugel." He passed a tray of squares of baked noodles.

Judge Kahane wondered about getting the mind into alpha state to be receptive to the powers of the universe, but he wasn't yet ready to pursue the concept. He'd ask Ursula more about it privately. In the meantime, the dinner discussion fell into the conventions of asking Ursula how she liked living at the Rose Plaza, why she chose Portland.

Judge Kahane added the connection to the ladies of the Mystery Club. He omitted his impression that they functioned more like a cabal than just women with a common interest in mysteries written by women. He didn't know them well enough to make any solid judgments.

Chapter Eighteen

Judge Kahane waited until Joel dropped them off at the Rose Plaza after the dinner before reminding Ursula that he wanted to learn more about the Wiccas' method for meditation.

"Can you come tomorrow afternoon?"

"It's Saturday. I'll be in synagogue all morning. Maybe after mincha."

"What's mincha?"

"It's the afternoon prayers. How about after sunset?"

"Fine. That will give me time to read some of this," she said, holding up Mattie's copy of the Kaplan book.

"Seven thirty?"

"Fine."

The Rose Plaza was a big complex. They parted at the elevator. Kahane got off at the second floor where he would then walk to the sky bridge and across to the Heights elevators, while Ursula continued up to the twelfth floor in the Tower.

At the appointed time Kahane showed up at Ursula's door. Her studio apartment still had a fragrance of sandalwood from a brass incense burner on the window sill. She showed the Judge a diagram of the phases of mental activity, Beta, Alpha, Theta and Delta. In all there were twenty-four levels, but the central part was the alpha, and it was divided into the primary colors of the rainbow, represented by the old mnemonic device, "Roy G. Biv," standing for Red, Orange, Yellow, Green, Blue, Indigo, and Violet, the of the spectrum you see in a rainbow. "You are supposed to visualize the colors in sequence. It's a sort of a count down."

"Sounds like self hypnosis to me." Kahane said.

"Maybe it is."

They were sitting on her small couch, just big enough for two, but as large as you could put into the cramped studio apartment. She had moved the glass topped coffee table, so they were sitting with their feet inside the magic circle in the throw rug she had bought at the New Age witches' store.

"The circle is part of the ritual," she explained. "The circle encloses the energy. I think it helps to separate us from outside sensual interference."

"Have you done that?"

"Not yet, but I think it will help me with my kabala meditation."

"Are you sure you want to pursue that? If you're getting into kabala you should be cautious. You need a guide."

Ursula looked at him over her granny glasses. "Could you guide me?"

"Kabala is not my thing. Let's say for me it's like mountain climbing. I don't climb because I'm afraid I'd fall off." He didn't add "because I'm ninety and happy enough to be able to walk the four blocks inside the Plaza to my apartment."

"Do you think Mattie would be my guide?"

Kahane shook his head. "I'm afraid I don't know her that well, It's a subject that's never come up. Some things you keep to yourself."

"There's a similarity. The Wiccas count down and the Kabbalists count up."

"What do you mean by that?"

Ursula explained, "The Wiccas use meditation to get down to the least static, if you could call it that, to the basic level of the mind. The Kabbalists seem to want to ascend to the Keter."

Kahane wanted to discourage her from taking those dangerous paths. "If you need a hobby, why not take up knitting? We have several knitters here."

She was offended at the suggestion.

Kahane backtracked and tried to justify his suggestion. "I think that concentration on knitting is a good way to blot out the outside world and withdraw."

"I don't want to blot out the outside world. I want to understand it, or rather the universe we are a part of."

"You mean like God?"

She didn't know. What was God? It was a subject neither was ready to explore, like what is the meaning of life?

How much easier it would be for her if Ursula simply "found Jesus", a state of mind Kahane found superficial. As William James had written, there were different paths to the mystical experience except James had left out Judaism, assuming wrongly that New Covenant Christianity was the fulfillment or completion of the Old Covenant. Ursula wanted something else, but Kahane didn't think she knew herself what it was.

Chapter Nineteen

IF Judge Kahane were going to discuss kabala intelligently with Ursula he'd better do some homework. His library in the big Heights apartment was limited. He'd disposed of his law library, which included hundreds of books. Nowadays those were reduced to digital files accessible from the mysterious data cloud. His limited bookshelf held a chumash, the standard Orthodox prayer book, and a Tanach, the Jewish translation of the Hebrew Bible. There were also titles by Jewish authors including Kafka's *The Trial*, a suitable book for a judge, but nothing about Kabala.

He turned to the Wikipedia and Google and was immediately overwhelmed. There were hundreds of hits, the downside of having access to too much information. Sorting through it was a challenge.

He recognized the diagram of the so-called "Tree of Life" which existed in various permutations from different cultures. It was not just a metaphysical Jewish thing. The tree of life diagram was used by many schools of meditation. The diagram had eleven connected circles, and each was described as a gate, each guarded by an angel. The gates represented various levels of awareness. Next to the top was chochma, wisdom, and at the very top the keter, or throne of God.

As Ursula said, it seemed one philosophy counted down, the other up. It sounded a bit like what Ursula described as the Wicca levels of the mind, the count down through the colors of the rainbow. It was like filtering out noise interference on an old AM radio. He thought what she described was similar to self hypnotism, put yourself into a trance.

The idea of cabala's stages being like guarded gates one had to pass through rang a bell. In his library was a collection of Jewish short stories including "Before the Law," by Kafka about a man who stood outside a gate waiting to get in, but never did. It was symbolic and subject to a lot of interpretation, but seen from a kabalistic point of view, that gate might have been one of those hurdles in the Tree of Life meditation. Made sense.

Had Kafka been a Kabbalist? Or a frustrated one? That kind of frustrating introspection struck Kahane as a gate not to wisdom but to frustration and madness like what happened to one of Elie Wiesel's friends.

Kahane didn't want Ursula to think herself into some sort of catatonic state. He feared she was in danger, but he was a judge, not a psychologist, and didn't know how to help..

Mattie was right. Ursula had triggered his old penchant for coming to the aid of people whose lives were messed up. Unfortunately, he didn't know how to go about it. Dabbling with Kabala was like playing catch with a hand grenade. You wouldn't know when it might go off.

Kahane's instinct was right. Ursula was stuck. She phoned the Wicca women at the New World store. "I need help," she said. "I'm having trouble, but I don't know why. Can you come over?"

They would. Their store was usually open until six but Carol and Hannah could close early and come after 5:00, depending on the notorious Portland rush hour traffic.

As it happened, this time it was Roberta Nelson who was volunteering at the front desk. There was no mistaking the bizarre garb of the two Wiccans and their white-faced, Goth-like makeup. While they signed in and got their visitor's badges Roberta phoned Ursula to tell her she had visitors.

Roberta's curiosity and animosity gnawed at her. She wished she were invisible and could eavesdrop on what those witches were up to. When she handed out meals at her church she saw plenty of odd characters, the dirty and the homeless, but this pair was beyond all her tolerance. Maybe it was because the people she saw at the church were needy. It gave her self satisfaction to feed them, but the act of charity was also a reinforcement of her own superiority. No wonder the recipients of charity also resented the givers.

Ursula's witchy visitors needed no charity.

It was ironic that Roberta was comfortable standing behind the counter at her church, dishing out food for the poor, homeless, and unwashed but did not like to sit beside them on the busses. That's why, when she could get it to start, she always drove her car.

Upstairs on the twelfth floor, Ursula let the two Wiccans in. She had put on a pot of coffee and opened a packet of Pims chocolate cookies. You had to serve something.

Carol, the taller and heavier of the pair, shrugged off her cape and got right down to business. "Something's bothering you."

"I'm stuck. I just can't seem to get through the visualizations."

Hannah closed her eyes and concentrated. At length, she took a deep breath and let it out slowly. "We need a magic circle."

Ursula indicated her rug with the pentacle design.

Carol saw the black candle on the window sill, lit it with a butane lighter, and turned out the light. They formed a circle, arms locked with Ursula in the middle.

Ursula shivered. Her forehead was damp and the back of her neck felt chilled. She needed the support of the women who held her within the circle.

Hannah, the skinny partner, bowed her head in concentration and spoke in an unnatural voice. "Someone wishes you harm."

"Yes," Carol agreed. "I sense a strong force of evil."

"What do I do? Who is it?"

"I don't know, but I sense anger."

Hannah had received an impression, too. "I see something white, a white car. Do you know someone with a white car?"

Ursula didn't. Carol let her go and stepped out of the circle. "This is very serious. Be careful. Think only positive thoughts. I think we need the larger circle to cast a spell of protection. The solstice is tomorrow night. Frances is hosting the ceremony at her home. With all of us drawing down the power of the moon we can ask the Goddess to protect you."

"What should I do?"

"We'll pick you up. Take a shower. No perfumes or scents that might distract. Purge your mind of bad thoughts. Wear the cloak we sold you. We'll do the rest."

"How can I thank you?"

"We don't ask for thanks or for an offering. We appreciate the opportunity to be of service and to do good for others. That is what Wicca is all about."

Ursula accompanied them back downstairs. At the front desk, as her guests signed out, Ursula asked. "What time will you pick me up tomorrow?"

"Nine o'clock."

"What if it's raining?"

Carol smiled with reassurance. "Isn't it always raining in Portland? The goddess speaks through the rain."

Roberta Nelson watched all of this. So, tomorrow night, was it? "Never suffer a witch to live" went through her mind like a mantra. She knew from that medieval tract that all witches were evil and must be destroyed.

Chapter Twenty

At the appointed time the next evening, the magical night of the solstice, Ursula waited in the Rose Plaza lobby for the Wiccans to arrive. She didn't know that Roberta Nelson was out in the parking lot in her old, white Chevy, the engine idling, the car facing out and ready to go.

It was raining, not heavily, but enough to slow down the traffic and to make the pavement slick. Not all of the autumn leaves had been swept up and where they remained in the gutters and corners they formed a slippery coating that made driving treacherous.

Carol and Hannah were late, but at length the distinctive, pink SUV with its provocative bumper stickers pulled up in the breezeway and Ursula came out to meet them. The SUV was so high she had to struggle to hoist her small body up to get inside. She sat in the back, buckled up, and they were off.

There were several options for the drive to Lake Oswego. The most direct way was route 43 down Macadam Boulevard, but you had to thread your way down to the waterfront through the maze of side streets, briefly slipping onto the I-5, before exiting and then easing under the viaduct to the waterfront, but Carol didn't know that route. Instead she chose Barbur Boulevard, which was faster. You could cut off and make a sharp left turn across the oncoming traffic lane and get down to the parallel street. It was a risky turn, especially at night, in the rain, with oncoming traffic.

"I think we're being followed," Hannah said.

There was someone nearly tailgating the SUV. Carol flipped the rear view mirror to cut the glare of the headlights of the car following close behind. She sped up to make more distance and hit the turn signal to warn the following driver that she was slowing down for a left turn.

There it was—the intersection for the short cut. At that moment a spurt of rain spattered the windshield but she was too late to speed up the windshield wipers.

There were cars coming, the headlights flaring in the rain. Carol made the quick turn, the rear end sliding a bit, but under control. They were onto the side street that connected them with Hamilton and then Macadam, the route to Lake Oswego.

"I think you lost them," Hannah said, looking back.

Ursula asked, "Did you see who it was?"

Neither of the two Wiccans did. Carol was too concerned with driving in the rainy dark to look back.

The drive to Lake Oswego on the #43 on a rainy night was hazardous. The road was winding and hilly, with poor sight distances, several traffic lights not visible until the last minute, and no reflective lines to show the edge of the pavement. Ursula was glad she no longer drove. She had been postponing cataract surgery and the flare of the oncoming lights was blinding.

They arrived safely.

Francis Beaumont had already assembled most of the Wiccas before Carol and Hannah arrived. They were able to form the circle out on the patio, which was still wet. Mercifully, the rain had stopped, and there was even a hint that the clouds were breaking up. Portland, being in a valley between two mountain ranges and abutting on the Columbia River Gorge, was subject to fast changing weather and hard to predict. It was a challenge for the TV weathermen, but probably a lot more interesting for them that it would be in places where weather hardly changed at all.

Carol whispered to Ursula, "This is a protective shield ceremony." The ritual began. The Wiccas placed Ursula in the middle of the circle. They all had their wands, some of which were elaborate, even encrusted with jewels. Others were simple sticks.

Ursula tried to be calm. She tried to imagine the colors of the rainbow in turn, tried to get into the right mental state, but she was uncertain and afraid. She felt a tingling, like static electricity.

At length, Mrs. Beaumont raised her arms and the ritual ended. Slowly letting out a deep breath she said, "The threat to you is diminished." .

"I don't even know what it is," Ursula said. Was this all some sort of mumbo jumbo?

"Whoever wished you harm is no longer a threat."

"What does that mean?"

Mrs. Beaumont shook her head. "I tried to visualize the threat. I saw a white car."

"We were being followed by a white car," Hannah said, remembering.

"But not any more," Carol said. "We lost it up on Barbur."

"Maybe they changed their mind," Ursula suggested.

"Maybe they're dead," Mrs. Beaumont said. "We never wish anyone any harm. The most we can do is to divert evil energy away, to set up a field of protection."

"I hope you're right," Ursula said.

"Wicca is entirely benign," Carol said.

"It is," Mrs. Beaumont. "We can wish you good fortune. It has come to me."

"Oh?"

"The circle wished me good fortune. I have had financial difficulty since my divorce. Now I have been offered a job as a school counselor here in Lake Oswego." She smiled and winked at Ursula. "I wonder what they will think if they realize I'm a witch."

Carol cocked her head, a wise gesture. "Just keep thinking good thoughts."

Chapter Twenty-one

The accident was on the late channel six murder and mayhem news, the theme, as usual, accidents, arsons, shootings, and assaults. The junior news reporter, called out at a moment's notice, was on the scene wearing a rain jacket and holding a microphone. She described how an older car had been T-boned crossing the center line on Barbur Boulevard in a section of the road where the speed limit was forty. The driver was an elderly woman, not yet identified, pending notification of next of kin. It was a one minute story, followed immediately by another of a drive by shooting on Killingsworth in NE Portland, photos of bullet holes in a door.

By then most of the Plaza residents had gone to bed and didn't see the broadcast. It wasn't until the next morning that the photo of the crushed Chevy appeared in the Metro section of the Oregonian. Eventually the identification of the victim was made and the gossips at the Rose Plaza learned that Roberta Nelson, aged 86, had been killed.

Within hours the second floor chapel had a notice "Roberta Nelson," with the date of birth and death on the table that featured a cross, a menorah, and a small statue of Buddha. It was alongside a notice of the death of a hundred year old woman who had been in assisted living for so long that everyone had forgotten her. Death was in the nature of the Rose Plaza, the next to last address of most of the residents.

Nelson was a common name, so when Judge Kahane saw the piece in the paper he wasn't sure that the Roberta Nelson was the women who lived in the Rose Plaza until he checked with the front desk.

After the initial shock, Katherine Seller was suspicious. She called Sylvia Jessup. "What was Roberta doing driving out on Barbur Boulevard at night? She told me she didn't drive at night because of her cataracts. And she usually only drove to church or to the Safeway grocery store down on Jefferson. That's barely a mile away."

Sylvia suggested, "Who would have seen her leave the garage?"

"Nobody."

"The paper said she'd had the accident after nine o'clock. I can't imagine her shopping for groceries at that hour. Where could she have been going?"

It was seldom that Katherine Seller was stymied. Why Roberta was out and where she was going promised to be an unsolved mystery. She guessed that all that remained was a memorial service, if there was one. There wasn't always. Some residents had private funerals, and no public celebrations of life, as they were called. Did Roberta have any relatives?

Chapter Twenty-two

Ursula had never seen Roberta's car, didn't know she still drove. She saw from the picture in the newspaper that it was white, not typical, as the current color of choice was some variation of grey, and learned that it was Roberta Nelson who had been the driver. She felt a chill. It was Roberta from the Mystery Club, the woman who had quoted the bible, "Never suffer a witch to live." Roberta had reacted with hostility to Ursula's pentacle jewelry and her witches' cape. She took the Malleus tract seriously. It must have been Roberta who was following her and the Wiccas. Had they somehow hexed the woman?

Ursula had trusted Carol and Hannah and the other Wiccas to simply protect her with some sort of moon goddess energy. Protect, but not to kill. Was Roberta's death the result of some witches' curse?

If it was, had Ursula inadvertently, without malice, in total ignorance, caused this to happen? She knew from the meetings of the Mystery Club that Roberta was hostile to witches, witchcraft, and the very idea. Roberta had apparently believed all that nonsense in the *Malleus Maleficarum.*

As for the possible impact of the Wicca ceremony on Roberta's driving, that had happened after the accident, not before. There could be no connection.

Then she remembered that Roberta had been at the front desk when Carol and Hannah had come to help her with her visualizations and learned there was danger. She hadn't imagined that the danger might have come from Roberta. What could she have been thinking, to follow them in her car in the rain?

Maybe she wasn't thinking at all, but simply reacting. Or maybe she was curious, suspicious, wondering what Ursula and her friends were up to? But there was no malice in that, was there? If she were curious, why didn't she just ask? Ursula knew Roberta was hostile to witches, but why follow them in her car? What did she think would happen? She had no idea of Roberta's intention.

Then there was the accident. Ursula had nothing to do with Roberta's accident, yet she felt somehow responsible. It was all very confusing and distressing.

If the accident had been brought about by the spell Hannah and Carol had tried to cast to protect her when they were in her apartment, was that more than simply some sort of cosmic shield? Was it also a curse? If there was such a thing as a witches' curse, that was even more distressing. Ursula wasn't the type of person to curse anyone. She would talk to Hannah and Carol and maybe the Wicca in Lake Oswego to get an explanation.

She did not want Roberta's fatal accident to be on her own conscience. You didn't have to be pronounced guilty in a court if you condemned yourself.

What about the Judge? Perhaps he would have a legal opinion about whether cursing someone who then died was an act of homicide. Murder by curse? Sounded entirely like superstition or some sort of voodoo like sticking a pin in a doll. You could go to jail for mailing a black wooden coffin to your IRS agent. That was perceived by the law as a threat, but there had been no such thing in Roberta's case. No one had threatened anybody.

She phoned her Wicca friends at the New Age store and asked if they had seen the story in the newspaper. They'd hardly noticed. Car crashes, rollovers, pedestrian deaths, hit and runs, were so common that one glossed over those news items. The Oregonian looked like a rogues' gallery you used to see in the post office. One got the impression that Portland was a wild west, lawless place.

Hannah, the skinny, smaller woman of the pair, said there was nothing to Roberta's concern. Carol, on the other hand, tried a visualization, looked back in time to reconstruct the evening. The solstice celebration in Lake Oswego had indicated that there was no threat to Ursula, or that any threat that had existed had passed.

On closer examination, deeper reflection, yes, the white car's driver had been hostile, but it was not in Wiccan practice to cause an accident like that. It was likely that Roberta Nelson's hostility had so distracted her driving that she caused the accident herself. As Carol said, what goes around, comes around. Wish harm to someone else and it comes back at you. Curses, well they might be something for gypsies, but not for Wiccas.

Ursula wasn't into gypsy curses.

She still wasn't satisfied and called Ira Kahane. "Did you see the newspaper, the story of Roberta Nelson's accident?"

Kahane hadn't. It wasn't in the *New York Times,* the newspaper he preferred. He remembered Roberta, of course, from the Mystery Club meetings.

Ursula tried to explain. "Roberta was following us to the solstice ceremony when she got T-boned."

Kahane was confused. "Wait a minute. So you were going to a solstice ceremony? How do you know she was following you?"

"Carol had a visualization."

"Who's Carol?"

"One of the women from the New Age store where I bought my carpet."

"And she had a visualization? I don't understand."

"She and her partner are Wiccas. They do these things."

Kahane was skeptical. It was sounding more and more like Ursula was going off the deep end. "So?"

Ursula's breath was out of sync, it was as if she'd started jogging without first warming up. She wasn't breathing normally. "If someone were cursed, and then died, could the person who did the cursing be charged with a crime, like murder?"

"No."

"What about manslaughter?"

Kahane's voice took the patronizing tone of someone talking to a child. "What's nonsense, Ursula. Did you curse someone?"

"No."

"I don't understand the problem. Why don't you start over from the beginning?"

"I was trying to do the Wicca meditations, counting down through the colors of the rainbow. I was hoping to tune into the moon goddess. I know this sounds silly to you, but the Wiccas believe it."

"There are many devices for meditation," Kahane suggested. "So what happened?"

"I got this strange feeling of foreboding and I called the women at the New Age store. They came over to the Plaza and we did a little ceremony. They said someone wished me harm and they tried to cast a spell to protect me."

To Kahane it sounded like a lot of nonsense, but he was willing to humor Ursula. "Did that work?"

"Not to their satisfaction. So they invited me to a solstice event in Lake Oswego. That's where their leader lives."

"Then what?"

"It was all very interesting, very spiritually invigorating. They told me the danger had passed."

This was totally outside Judge Kahane's experience. It sounded to him like something you'd run into with a fortune teller who intended to separate you from your money. "Did they say what the danger was?"

"Yes. Someone driving a white car."

Kahane was silent.

"Roberta was driving a white car."

"There are a lot of white cars on the road, Ursula."

"But we were being followed by a white car until we turned off Barbur Boulevard. That's where the accident happened."

"I think you're letting your imagination run away with you."

"Roberta knew I was being picked up. And you know how she felt about witches."

"That still doesn't prove anything. You didn't cause her accident."

Ursula didn't sound reassured. "I was afraid one of the Wiccas put a curse on Roberta, but they insist that they don't do such things."

"Then you have nothing to worry about."

"Well, I do Ira." She didn't usually call him anything but Judge. "I now have a sense of what kind of prejudice the Wiccas go through. People like Roberta hate them."

"You already know that from the Malleus tract."

"Yes, but that's from the fifteenth century."

It reminded Judge Kahane of an old Jewish joke. "There's a story of a Jew in Vienna who asked a cab driver to take him to the synagogue. The cab driver beat him up. When the driver was taken to court the judge asked him why he attacked the Jew. 'The Jews killed Christ,' the cabbie said. 'But that was two thousand years ago,' the judge said. 'Yes, but I just heard about it yesterday.'"

Ursula didn't laugh.

"These old prejudices hang on," Kahane said. "Witches are always portrayed as evil, like the Wicked Witch of the West in the *Wizard of Oz*. Then there's Halloween. You never see a good witch. They're always portrayed as evil."

"That's not reality," Ursula said.

"And Jews are not all rich, money grubbing, and sneaky, but that's what many people think."

"That's not you, Ira."

"Yes, but you don't see me wearing a kippa except at my grandson's when we have a Sabbath meal. I don't wear it in public."

Ursula paused as she thought about that.

"And," the judge continued, "I wouldn't advise you to wear a witch's pointy hat down on Pioneer Square even though Portland prides itself on being weird. It confuses people."

That might have been the end of it, but the Mystery Club meeting was coming up, the first time Roberta wasn't there.

Chapter Twenty-three

Neither Judge Kahane nor Ursula had read the current mystery, so were unprepared for the Mystery Club meeting. Truth be told, the Judge had lost interest. At first it seemed like a good idea, a new direction in his reading, but after a career of real mysteries, court cases, and dealing with villainous perps, as the police called them, what he found in the cozy mysteries preferred by Katherine Seller to him was mere pap, and the stories contrived. No fiction could even come close to the realities he was used to.

Not only that, but he had taken a dislike to Katherine Seller. It wasn't her berets that irritated him but her bossy, vindictive nature. She had a mean streak. He wouldn't yet say she was an evil person. She was merely self-satisfied and controlling. He didn't need any of that. This meeting, he decided, would be his last.

Ursula followed his advice about not attracting undesirable attention and did not wear the pentacle pendent. Roberta's fatal accident had put a dark shadow on her flirtation with Wicca.

The cause of Roberta's accident and her motivation for being out in her car at that hour were unknown. Instead there was brief speculation about Roberta's next of kin. Sylvia Jessup said, "I think she has a son who retired to Florida."

Florida was at the opposite corner of the country. To fly in to PDX would mean a full day of travel, probably requiring a change in Chicago. Cross country flights were not only expensive. They were not as exhausting as eighteen hour flights to China or Japan or Australia, but not comfortable. What retired person had the stamina for such travel? Sylvia said she would never do it.

Someone would have to take charge of clearing out Roberta's apartment. Probably her furniture would end up in the Plaza's resale shop and, if no one wanted to buy it, the Salvation Army would pick it up. That was the pattern. Heirs would take whatever mementos they wanted. Items not claimed or saleable would simply be thrown away and the apartment put up for sale to a new tenant.

As they left the meeting Judge Kahane confided to Ursula, "I don't think I'll be coming to any more of these meetings."

"I won't either. I think somehow Katherine and Sylvia think I'm responsible for Roberta's accident."

Kahane reassured her, "That's only your guilty imagination."

As they waited for the elevator, he asked "Are you still going to pursue the Wicca thing?"

"I don't know."

"What about kabala? I suggested you consult my grandson's wife Mattie."

"I think kabala may be too difficult. I looked up that tree of life and those gates to the keter. Each is guarded by an evil angel."

Kahane wasn't into angels. In spite of the many references to angels in the Torah, what exactly angels were was a subject his coreligionists never got into. Angels, like the angel of death who provided Abraham with a ram to sacrifice instead of his son, were a mystery. His son had joked about having a guardian angel, but that was something so insubstantial in Judaism that it played no part. As for encounters with evil angels guarding the gates in the kabalistic tree of life, he wanted no part of it. "Deliver me from evil."

The elevator had arrived. Kahane wouldn't be getting on, as he had a long walk on the second floor to the sky bridge and his Heights apartment.

Ursula entered the elevator, but Kahane held his hand in front of the censor to keep the doors open. "It's in the 23rd psalm. 'Lead me in straight paths for His name's sake and deliver me from evil.'"

"I'll stick to the straight path, Ira. Thank you."

The elevator door closed.

The end

About Harley L. Sachs:

Though born in Chicago and raised in Indiana, Harley L. Sachs considers himself an international, having lived in Germany, Sweden, Scotland, and Denmark. He earned a degree in English at Indiana University, then served in the US Army in Germany. After getting his Master's degree at I.U. he returned to Europe and worked under cover for several years. He met and married Ulla in Stockholm, Sweden and they spent a year's honeymoon in a Scottish castle. Returning to the USA, Sachs taught English briefly at Southern Illinois University then moved to Michigan Technological University in the Upper Peninsula where he and his wife raised three daughters. He took early retirement and now lives in Portland, Oregon.

Harley L. Sachs is the author of many novels, short stories, magazine articles and newspaper columns. His short stories have been broadcast on the BBC World Service short wave and on Oregon Public Radio's Golden Hours. His awards for writing are too numerous to list as are his over 1000 publications.

If you enjoyed this Mystery Club novel you may wish to read others in the series. See below.

MYSTERY NOVELS

The Mystery Club Series

THE MYSTERY CLUB SOLVES A MURDER
First and most popular of the Mystery Club series. Mary Higgins finds the body of Dora Reed on the roof of the Plaza retirement building, notifies the police, then tells the Mystery Club. They assume several suspects: the manager of the Plaza, Dora's son Donald, or a Plaza employee. Dora's husband, Ed Sutherland, is in Hawaii on board the yacht Miss Chief with an all girl crew. Carrying on their own investigation, the Mystery Club finally suspects Sutherland, though he seems to have a perfect alibi. If they can prove it to their satisfaction, will a court ever convict him-- if he can be found somewhere in the Pacific?

THE MYSTERY CLUB AND THE DEAD DOCTOR
Third in the popular Mystery Club series. The Mystery Club consists of five elderly women who live at the Rose Plaza and discuss mysteries written by women. The Mystery Club ladies have no idea of the consequences when Viola Cartwright, their blind member, asks them to go over her Medicare bills. That leads to suspicion about the identity of her personal assistant, Dorothy Anderson, who turns out to be using a stolen identity. Viola's doctor runs a phony clinic owned by a member of the Russian Mafia. Soon the investigation of Medicare bills leads to murder and tragedy, stopped only by the courage of Mary Higgins.

THE MYSTERY CLUB AND THE HIDDEN WITNESS
Fourth in the Mystery Club series. The ladies of the Mystery Club they discover one of the residents is a crook under WITSEC, the witness protection program. He apparently keeps dipping into the employee gift fund. The Mystery Club bands together to track down the missing money, but what they discover is danger.

THE MYSTERY CLUB AND THE SERIAL WIDOW
Fifth in the Mystery Club series. Caroline Kostinsky, new resident at the Rose Plaza, is a widow four times over and she's looking for a fifth husband in retired General Hardcastle, but when drunk she says she killed all of her husbands. Except for her confession, there's no evidence. Now what?

DELIVER ME FROM EVIL
Two newcomers to the Mystery Club are the diminutive Ursula Besette and ninety-year old Judge Ira Kahane. Ursula is a new Rose Plaza resident who is at a crossroads in her life and is interested in Wicca and kabala as a means to a new equilibrium, but there is danger in her investigations.

WHITE SLAVE
Sequel to *The Mystery Club Solves a Murder* which ended with the prime suspect, Ed Sutherland, lost overboard from the yacht Miss Chief during a Pacific storm. Two years later, Detective Casey learns that Sutherland's valuable gold bracelet has turned up in Portland in a pawn shop. Casey tracks it down, but hits a dead end. He doesn't know that Sutherland was rescued by a Korean slave fishing boat, the Oyang 70 where he is forced to work under unspeakable conditions. When the Oyang sinks, he is stranded in New Zealand. He is penniless and ill, has no clothes, no passport and has been reduced to utter misery. He cannot stay in New Zealand, and if he returns to Oregon he is sure to be arrested. What then? Conviction for First Degree murder? A death sentence? Can there be any redemption for this not very nice man?

The Irwin Glass Series

BETRAYAL
Prequel to **Retribution**. Irwin Glass, BA in Russian, MA in International Relations, has a promising career in the Foreign Service in Moscow until he is snared in a classic "honey pot" seduction. He's young and naïve, honest, always wants to do the right thing, but at every turn he is betrayed. The incident in Moscow destroys his career. He is accused of being a paid Soviet agent and is pursued by the consequences of his encounter with the KGB twenty years later. Some enemies never let go

RETRIBUTION

Sequel to **Betrayal.** Newly married to Ivy Hartshorn, Irwin Glass gets a dunning letter from the IRS for taxes on interest at the Washington, DC account he didn't think he had. It's a joint account with his missing birth daughter and the balance is huge. Assuming it's money Katya's KGB father of record, Vladimir Putinsky (now Putin) deposited for her living expenses, Irwin moves it to force her to contact him. But Ivy warns him that he is laundering money and the people it belongs to will come after him. Irwin's complicated life is catching up with him, but this time he will find retribution.

BURNT OUT

Irwin Glass is approached by FBI Agent Wilkins who asks for Irwin's lists of foreign students. Not satisfied he wants more and is looking for potential terrorists among the Moslem students. Gradually Irwin is sucked into the role of FBI informant on the Michigan Institute of Technology's Muslim Students' Association and the results are tragic.

Other Mysteries

MURDER BY MAIL (previously SCRATCH OUT!)

German exchange student Klaus Hitz is more interested in making money than in asking questions about his work assignment. He doesn't know that the industrialist father of his punk girl friend is using him in a terrorist conspiracy to kill everyone in the United States with a mass mailing of a scratch and sniff virus. The plot begins to unravel when a Polish nurse brings blood samples from Libya and alerts a CIA agent. While the CIA and FBI track down the terrorists, Klaus Hitz gradually figures it out. How can he avoid being murdered or imprisoned for being naive?

MURDER IN THE KEWEENAW

CIA agent recovering from Post traumatic Stress after failed missions in Finland and a divorce is fishing in Lake Superior when he snags a corpse. He thinks he has seen the girl before and his attempt to identify her leads him to a ring of deadly pornographers. It almost costs him his own life.

CONSPIRACY!
Technical writer Tom Godot can't believe his luck when CONSPIRACY!, the book he has co-written with the elusive Harold Stevenson, is a hit. The book details a plot to hijack communication satellites. As Tom crosses the country on his book tour, he is disturbed by people interested in early drafts and dogged by an NSA agent. Communicating by fax with his editor and by encrypted e-mail with the mysterious Stevenson, Tom reaches out in his loneliness to his California girl friend Sylvia Hanson who turns out to be a pivotal figure. There is another conspiracy, and Tom is part of it

THE GOLD CHROMOSOME
When Adam Rottman's childless Aunt Sadie Gold died, the eight cousins learned her estate was in an irrevocable trust, the proceeds going to Adam's sister Sarah while she lives. After Sarah's death, the money would go to the last surviving cousin. It's a fatal tontine Adam's lawyer brother Harold set up. Would the cousins kill each other for one million dollars? Sarah's car is found in the river, but not Sarah. That begins a series of mysterious deaths. Coincidence? Or Murder? Who will be next? Adam and his psychologist wife Deborah must stop the chain before he, too, is eliminated.

BEN ZAKKAI'S COFFIN
Born of a Jewish father and a Catholic mother, Herman Bachrach insists he has no religion, but he is drawn by circumstance into a holocaust vendetta over gold stolen by a Swiss bank from Jewish depositors. Seduced by a woman who calls herself Diana, no last name, Herman is suspected by detective Sheehan to be her murderer. Someone else wants him dead. His Jewish boss provides him with a lawyer, but sends him to Switzerland to finish the job "Diana" started. It's an assignment he can't refuse. The result is an epiphany of identity that changes Herman's life forever.

THE LOLLIPOP MURDER
A warning for wannabe novelists! What happens when a stable of neurotic novelists who live in their pseudonyms and are bound by iron clad contracts are invited aboard their miserly Florida publisher's yacht for the Miami Book Fair only to find that they have no hope of ever earning a dime of royalties for their books? All this as Hurricane Gerta

threatens to sink the yacht at the dock.   It's grounds for murder

SCI-FI AND FANTASY

NEVER TRUST A TALKING HORSE
The narrator of this dystopian novel escapes preventive detention into a world he discovers has gone mad.   Hungry, he is told he can eat for free at Lachumba's supper club, only to discover that he might be the main dish.   He rescues Iris I.   Iris from the ovens and in a series of episodes explores the insane world in search of a livelihood.   He gradually realizes why he was incarcerated in the first place, but by then it is too late.   His and Iris's roles have been reversed.   Arrested, they are given a sadistic sentence which is their final challenge.

THE SEARCH FOR JESSE BRAM
Jesse Bram, the young hero of this metaphysical science fiction adventure, is unaware of his Jewish roots.   An Eldre of mixed breed, he is marooned on the post apocalyptic shunned planet URth where technology and books have been destroyed.   The URthlings variously view Jesse as a bringer of cargo for the half-breed prefect Hrod, as the reborn Savior by crypto-Christians, and as a link to the past by a remnant of Jews.   The Galactic Federation suspects him of treason and he is pursued by an enigmatic Trinian policeman.   If Jesse survives, will he be convicted? If acquitted, what next?

SHORT STORIES

THREADS OF THE COVENANT: THE JEWS OF RED JACKET
A collection of twenty-one short stories about Jewish life in small town America centering about two main characters, David Katz, the only Jewish boy in Red Jacket, and Richard Goldman, the only Jewish professor at Copper country Community College. Each story depicts another aspect of what it means to be a Jew in a small town as each character comes to realize his own identity.

MISPLACED PERSONS
Though set in different locales what these stories have in common is a central character who is out of his element, in the wrong place, coming to grips with cultural, generational, or physical displacement.   In

PROBLEM FOR THE TEACHER an expatriate fumbles for a living; in LIMBO an ex-G.I. is adrift in Copenhagen; in TRIUMPH OF THE WILL a nervous wreck seeks recuperation; in MISCALCULATION a would be tax evader succumbs to his own fears; in THE LIE a drunk gets himself into difficulties, and in THE GIRLS OF FREDERIKSHAVN an old man is trapped by girls looking for action.

YOOPER TALES AND OTHER FUNNY STUFF
Extracted from the massive volume of Sachs's published Essays and Columns: 1992-2011, this collection of stories related to Michigan's Upper Peninsula, known as the UP, home of Yoopers, reveals the truth about snow fleas, ice worms, the humungous fungus (world's largest living things) and the rigors of winters in the remote north woods. You can also learn how to catch and cook the Mosquito Giganticus and why visitors won't come. Sachs has several awards for his humor.

AHOY! QUARTERDECK!
Originally published as IRMA QUARTERDECK REPORTS but re-released with new illustrations and, in the paperback edition, with sea shanties, this funny book is a series of boating anecdotes about Irma and her bumbling husband Ralph ("I can't believe I lost the anchor") Quarterdeck in their many boating adventures and mishaps. One reviewer says the book is as informative as Chapman's famous manual, but more fun. Readers will find plenty of laughs in this book and at the same time learn a great deal of boating fundamentals.

ANNA-LENA'S TROLL AND OHER STORIES
Each of the three Sachs daughters has a story in this children's book. "Anna-Lena's Troll" explores the nature of trolls, which represent the dark side of human behavior as Anna-Lena's nasty letter to Santa is rewarded by the gift of a nasty troll. "The Return of Baby Suzy" is the true story of Cynthia's worn out doll and its resurrection. "The Stars for Christmas" is the remarkable surprise Belinda got along with her new eye glasses. Other family stories are Christmas related.

NON-FICTION

FREELANCE NONFICTION ARTICLES

This third edition of a monograph on freelance writing first published by the Society for Technical Communication is newly updated. This little manual provides tips for interviewing, article structure, article preparation and submission, photography, and business practice.

Both FREELANCE NONFICTION ARTICLES and *Chilly-Chilly-BANG! How we Freelanced Through Europe's Coldest Winter in a VW with a Kid* are combined in a double volume, *The Writing Life*.

"IS"

As Bill Clinton said, "It all depends on what the meaning of "is" is."
A problem we all have is distinguishing between what is real and what is not. This is in fact an age-old question. This volume switches between classical instances of the problem to the author and his psychiatrist and his wife. What is real? That all depends on the meaning of "real."

MEMOIRS

THE MISADVENTURES OF CPL. SACHS

Convinced that asthma would keep him out of the army, Sachs was disappointed to be drafted. He was unfit for combat, and was placed in an experimental basic training unit called Queer Company. Later he ended up as a company clerk in Heidelberg. There began his own version of a Grand Tour.

THE 1957 SACHS ARCTIC EXPEDITION

Memoir of a hitchhiking adventure as ex-GI Harley Sachs, studying in Stockholm, Sweden on the GI Bill, sets off hitchhiking to North Cape, the northernmost point in Europe in search of the midnight sun.. Illustrated.

FROM TENT TO CASTLE: MEMOIR OF A YEAR LONG HONEYMOON

Setting off from Stockholm, Sweden on rebuilt one speed bicycles, Harley and Ulla embarked on an open-ended honeymoon with no fixed destination and equipped with a tent, a thin double sleeping bag, a tiny gasoline stove, and $3000. After arriving in Britain, Ulla discovered she was pregnant. Tired of unrelenting rain, they advertised for a cheap place to spend the winter. They were offered the gatehouse to Borthwick Castle outside Edinburgh, Scotland for $25 a month by British author Theo Lang.

CHILLY-CHILLY-BANG—HOW WE FREELANCED THROUGH EUROPE'S COLDEST WINTER IN A VW WITH A KID

Companion piece to *Freelance Nonfiction Articles.*   The former is a how to book.   This is a "how we did it" memoir.   The author knew nothing about Volkswagens when they set off, but as they worked from VW dealer to dealer getting the old Combi fixed, he learned! It's as much a book for VW enthusiasts as it is for writers.

QUEER COMPANY

Not a gay novel, this is a fictionalized memoir of an experimental basic training unit at the end of the Korean War.   All the draftees were physically unfit for combat but the army didn't want to discharge them. Instead they got modified training in a company unfortunately designated Q.   In the Army phonetic alphabet Q is Queen, but Q company was called queer.   A copy is in the US Army historical archives.

CARTOONS

HUNTING THE MAIL BUOY AND OTHER HAZARDS TO NAVIGATION

Cartoons originally intended for the US Navy newspaper. Inspired by the works of Mike Payton..

www.ingramcontent.com/pod-product-compliance
Lightning Source LLC
Chambersburg PA
CBHW051843170626
46807CB00003B/1331